M000043083

COBALT CHRONICLES

COBALT CHRONICLES

a novel by

Kathryn Den Houter

MISSION POINT PRESS

Readers are encouraged to go to
www.MissionPointPress.com to
contact the author or to find
information on how to buy this
book in bulk at a discounted rate.

MISSION POINT PRESS

Published by Mission Point Press
2554 Chandler Rd.
Traverse City, MI 49686
(231) 421-9513
www.MissionPointPress.com

ISBN: 978-1-950659-44-9
Library of Congress Control Number: 2020902725

Printed in the United States of America.

ALSO BY
KATHRYN DEN HOUTER

Abigail's Exchange

*Resilience: A Workbook, Powering Through
Adversity to Find Happiness*

Van: A Memoir of My Father

DEDICATION

This novel is dedicated to Tom Pine (1946 - 2019), my first editor. His unconditional support and irrepressible humor fostered my development as a writer. Now, he is living the eternal story, but he is sorely missed!

CONTENTS

INTRODUCTION

The inspiration for this book came from two sources. The first one was from the Hagar story in the Old Testament of the Bible. As a young girl, I was drawn to Hagar and fixated on how she might have felt being caught between Sarah and Abraham. Hagar was impregnated by Abraham and then, targeted by Sarah. The turmoil and confusion she suffered was not unlike what Esy experienced with Stella. Forced to live in a desert, Hagar was ordered to return to Sarah and Abraham's household and submit to her mistress.

There are similarities between Hagar and Esy, but I dwelled on this one question: What are the differences between Hagar, who is under the law of the Old Testament and Esy who has experienced the transforming love of Christ found in the New Testament? Three of Esy's behaviors indicate her freedom in Christ: 1.) reconciliation between Stella and her, 2.) Esy's attempts to forgive those who exploit her, and 3.) her determination to rise above the servant-role to claim her freedom. These actions are distinctly different from Hagar in the Old Testament.

The other source of inspiration was my trip to Africa in January of 2018. The African people are remarkable—they express joy in the face of horrific hardship. The Spirit is moving throughout Africa. They connect with each other, they seize every moment to rejoice, they are playful, and grateful for love from others. Their hearts are open. I yearn for a better life for them—a life without poverty, exploitation, and violence. I want every child to have the opportunity of an education, better medical care and sufficient food.

Cobalt Chronicles shines a spotlight on forced child labor, human trafficking and sexual assault against women in the Democratic Republic of the Congo. This novel takes one individual and follows her life from the first exploitation in the mine, to the obstacles she confronts to get an education, to the frustrating trap of prostitution and victimization of sexual assault. Finally, the deficiency of the medical care with extended wait-times is a critical problem—it cries for a solution. Twelve percent of the children in the DRC do not make their first birthday.

The harsh environment took its toll on Esy's body. Her life is a short one, a mere forty years from 1947 to 1987. In spite of these unfair odds, Esy is a strong, resourceful young woman who manages to salvage her life of suffering by leaving a generation-changing legacy. It is a powerful and healing story.

My hope is that you will identify with Esy, feel her pain, and experience deeper compassion for the African women.

Kathryn Den Houter
January 12, 2020
kathryndenhouter@gmail.com
kathryndenhouter.com

PROLOGUE

The Belgian Congo had been targeted for exploitation for a long time. It is rich in natural resources, but its rank on the human development scale is one of the lowest. The Congolese people have not benefited from their wealth. Despite all of its potential abundance, the people of the Congo are subjected to widespread injustice from their own government and from capitalists abroad. Rape, sickness and poverty are everywhere and their children are not protected. Children endure long workdays and dangerous working conditions.

Historically, The first wave of destruction came from the slave trade, which was followed by the wholesale killing of their elephants for their ivory. Next, during the "red rubber era," the world's rapacious appetite for rubber because of rubber tires all but destroyed the people of the Congo. Today, the Democratic Republic of the Congo is a marginalized country that provides over half the world's supply of cobalt. Much of the cobalt comes from forced child labor where children are not provided an education and a normal childhood is denied them.

Cobalt is a precious metal and is used for lithium batteries, which are integral to high tech industries. It's also used in magnetic steels, high-speed cutting tools, and in alloys used in jet turbine generators. James Conca in his article, *Blood Batteries* in Forbes Magazine says, "Unfortunately, the demand for cobalt is increasing like a bacte-

ria culture in a petri dish, and poor children are its food."
Despite all this natural wealth, the people of the Congo
continue to suffer—there is no end it sight.

ℭℜℭℜℭℜ

The Belgian Congo before 1947, when Esy was born was
a chaotic place. How could one expect to have stability
when greed and unrestrained exploitation was the mode
of operation? The country proved rich in natural resources, potentially one of the richest in the world and this
caught the eyes of European industrialists who raped the
natural wealth of this African nation, forcing its people
into servitude. The clash of the European and African
cultures created a country that was chopped up into
small sections like a crazy quilt, which was done to max-
imize profits.

In 1877, Henry Stanley signed a five-year contract with
the Belgian King Leopold to explore the Congo. This
meant he slashed his way across Central Africa, killing
anyone who got in his way. From the exploration, King
Leopold II was able to seize the territory and shamelessly
ravage the land and exploit its indigenous people. His
ravenous appetite for wealth and recognition grew like a
cancer on the land. Leopold laid claim to what became the
Congo Free State. *Free* was the moniker used because he
touted the virtues of free trade, which became an induce-
ment to future entrepreneurs. For Leopold, the principles
of free trade meant no taxes, no tariffs, no quotas, and no
restrictions. It was a reckless, profit-driven scheme.

Poachers hunted the elephants for their ivory tusks
and ripped herds of these animals away from the African landscape. The result of this slaughter saturated the

ivory markets and the profits for trading ivory dwindled to nothing. This made King Leopold unhappy, forcing him to conjure up another scheme.

In the late 1800s, John Boyd Dunlop invented the pneumatic tires used for bicycles. Within twenty years, the price of rubber shot up four times. Leopold seized the opportunity to invest and ultimately exploit the plentiful rubber crops in the Congo. What evolved from this escapade was a brutality that was unparalleled in the African countries and throughout the world.

Leopold's rubber scam began when he raised a private army, which he referred to as the Force Publique. Villagers became the work force and Force Publique the enforcers. They demanded—without exception—a fixed quota of fifty large pails of liquid rubber. If the workers fell short, the enforcers exacted cruel and severe punishment. The army expected absolute compliance.

Floggings, shootings, and rapes by the Force Publique happened often and capriciously. The smell of death skulked through the dark forests secretly and unannounced. The helter-skelter and unprecedented brutality was so rampant that it earned the term *hecatomb*, which is worse than *genocide* because of its wholesale destruction. Killings were random and actuated with a total disregard for life, whereas a genocide kills a targeted population. Sudden streaks of murdering were as routine as eating and sleeping.

Since bullets were at a premium, the captains made sure the sentries were doing their job and not using the bullets by shooting game for sport. The officers required their subordinates to cut off a hand of those they killed to prove they put the bullet to good use. Men and women would feign death while their hand was being lopped off. For a generation, many people in the Congo could be seen roaming the countryside minus a hand. The reign of Leopold II and his bloodstained policies became known as the "red rubber era."

The Congolese people became numb to the horrific atrocities. The putrid smell of rotting flesh hung in the air from victims' intestines being strung on trees. Heads of little babies were impaled on stakes to set an example. Like a malignant tumor, the culture of death destroyed every inch of human decency.

Day after day, the villagers toiled in the forests of the Western Congo, tapping the trees, and watching the milky substance trickle out. The latex had a terrible smell when exposed to the air and warmed by the sun. As coagulation and degradation occurred, it gave off a rank odor. The laborers breathed and worked in this stench all day, every day.

Mosquitos infested the dark black interior of the forest, which created a hotbed for malaria and sleeping sickness. Contaminated streams and water holes spread other diseases. Fear from retaliation for missing quota, the foul odor of the rubber, and the hot humid air prompted many to run farther into the forest away from the sentries, but the enforcers hunted them down. Once found, punishment was severe. Initially, Leopold's fortune increased due to the demand and escalating price of rubber, but his greed destroyed the Congolese people. Some estimate the rubber scam in the Congo caused the deaths of eight to ten million villagers.

As Marlow said in Joseph Conrad's *Heart of Darkness,* "The conquest of earth, which mostly means taking it away from those who have a different complexion or slightly flatter noses than ourselves, is not a pretty thing when you look into it too much." Conrad concluded that there was a thin line between civility and barbarism.

The Force Publique, Leopold's colonial army, was under the firm leadership of white officers. Half of the King's budget was spent maintaining his army, which grew to more than five thousand Belgians, mercenaries, and Africans. The other monies went for the development of the City of Leopoldville, which later became known as Boma. Here he built houses with European facades, a narrow-gauge railroad through the rough interior, and seaports that would carry precious cargo across the Atlantic Ocean to ports in the west.

The world heard about the horrors of King Leopold's policies, but they did nothing. Many dismissed the assaults as the price of doing business and viewed these atrocities as necessary to insure profitable trading to more "civilized" countries. The Congo was considered a financial enterprise, not a colony.

Having squandered all of his family's wealth and the money he borrowed from the Belgian government, King Leopold II came up empty-handed. His schemes were reckless and in the final analysis, unsustainable. The elected officials of the Belgian government took control of the Congo in 1908 and changed the name from the Congo Free State to the Belgian Congo. At that point, the Congo shifted from being a mere financial enterprise to a colony. Although colonization further mired African identity, mission schools were a positive outcome. Children were taught to read, speak languages, learn math, and understand the world around them. From 1908 to the late 1950s there was a "peaceful" stability. In other words, the Congolese people accepted their subservient role. It turned out, however, to be a calm between two stormy periods.

CHAPTER 1

Mama Mary

ଓଃଓଃଓଃ

My name is Esynama. They call me Esy. My life's story is as treacherous and serpentine as the mighty Congo River. I want you to know me and see what I've seen.

"Psst, Esy!" Moyo whispered, as he jostled her awake. Disoriented, Esy opened her eyes to a presence so close she could feel warm breath on her face. Startled, Esy sat up, surprised to see her brother.

"Is that you, Moyo?" she asked.

"Yes," he said softly. "Mama wants you to come home—she's dying."

Jarred by his message, she leaped out of bed just as she saw Moyo tiptoe around the dingy cots to exit the tent. Thankfully, Mama had given him clear directions to find her—"she'll be in the first tent behind the row of grass huts," she had said. Esy dressed posthaste, grabbed a plantain for her journey, and held her breath to evade the children's coughs from disease and cobalt dust. She peered out of the tent to check her surroundings. Suddenly, just two huts away, the light in Big Boss's shed switched on, piercing the dark. Startled, Esy took off in a sprint, looking behind her just long enough to see him charge out the door. Esy's adrenaline surged, forcing her legs to move faster. She leaped over the fence and caught the edge of her dress on the wire. Frantically, she yanked the cloth off the barbed wire pressing her left leg into the sharp blades. Wincing with pain, she jerked her leg free and with one mad dash, she jumped down and loped through the bushes to get out of harm's way. As she ran away she felt a trickle of blood running down her leg.

"I must run! I must hurry!" Esynama whispered. "Moyo risked his life to tell me Mama Mary was dying. I will run to hold and kiss her one more time."

"Psst, Esy, I'm over here behind the big tree," Moyo whispered.

"I hurt my leg—go ahead of me. Get home as fast as you can. I'll catch up when I can," Esy ordered. She stopped long enough to look down at her wound, tore off the hem of her dress and wrapped her injury. She kept on running.

Death was rampant in the mining camp of the Katanga Province in the Congo. Dysentery and Hard Metal Lung Disease (HMLD) were to blame. The cobalt dust aggravated lung tissue to such an extent that a virulent hacking cough filled the night air. Big Boss erected a fence around the camp to keep the workers in the camp since some tried to escape during the night. Big Boss needed every worker to keep his mine profitable. Hearing rustling in the huts and tents alarmed him and he used whatever means he had to secure his encampment.

Esy forced her legs to move faster, then faster. The inky black night showed only a half moon, but it was a cloudless sky and enough to light her way. The rivulets from the heavy rains rough cut the road but the thick callouses on her feet served her well as she made her way through the rills and gullies. As she rounded a bend, she heard a gunshot ring out behind her. She stopped running, frozen in fear, her heart racing. She craned her neck to see where the gunfire was coming. It seemed to be ahead and above her. *Did he shoot my dear brother Moyo?* Listening for a cry or a moan, Esy heard only the sound of heavy feet tromping on the path and rustling brush nearby.

Then she saw him—Big Boss standing high on a knoll. She could see his silhouetted face, shadow black against the moonlight. He held a pistol, which flashed in the moon's glow.

Esynama's heart was filled with terror as she hid in the darkness of a bank's cutaway. The suspense of that moment felt like an eternity. She held her breath. To her relief, Big Boss turned around and with an exasperated huff, stomped through the brush, his footsteps fading in the distance.

Hiding in silence, she thought about her Mama. It had been a long time since she had seen her. Esy didn't want to leave her mama and go to the mine but it was her father, Daddy Dayana who had taken her away from home and forced her to work in the cobalt mines. She gave her hard earned money to her daddy and to Big Boss for her keep.

She stayed in hiding until she was sure he had gone back to camp. Carefully slipping out of her dark hiding place, she began running even faster as if the devil were chasing her. Thoughts swirled inside her head. *Is Moyo okay? Is Mama still alive? Will Daddy Dayana be at Mama's house? Will he take me back to the mine to work for Big Boss?*

She didn't want to go back. Life in the mine was hard and Big Boss was cruel. He paid Daddy Dayana many francs for the work she did, and he kept the money— didn't give it to Mama or to his daughter. The only money Mama received was from the men who stopped by after supper. They gave her francs to feed her and Moyo. He was a good son when he stayed with Mama in their small hut. Mama was all alone in the country-side, eight kilometers from the Ruashi mine with only a small boy to take care of her. Esy never understood until later, why the twilight visitors were giving her francs.

Esynama panted and her bare feet stung from the hidden stones under the red earth. She was tired but she pressed on wanting to see her mother one last time. Esy remembered when Mama sang and hummed to her almost every night. "Sweet baby girl, your mama loves you. Surely you will find a happy life. Sunshine will follow you and make you smile."

Mama would sing solos when Esy was in bed, too. Mournful songs, filled with weeping words. Mama cared for Esy the best she could without anyone to take care of her needs. Gratefully, Esy remembered the good days before she became sick. Mama raised manioc in the backyard prying the soil loose to find thick tubers. Carefully, she lined them up to dry in the sun and then, after a few days, ground them into a flour-like powder. Mama's Belgian mother, Amelia, told her it was called tapioca in her country, a sweet treat for dessert. Daddy used to do his part making food for the family by climbing high into the palm trees and with his machete, chopping off bunches of greasy nuts. Then, he would press them until a lovely orange juice ran out. It looked like liquid copper. From the palm oil, he would make *mwambe* sauce for their rice and taro.

Those had been happy days when Mama and Daddy worked together. Sadly, Mama got sick and everything changed. Daddy changed too. He was disheartened and lured into gambling by scoundrels he called friends. This life sucked him in and the cost was huge—the loss of his moral compass. The money he and Esy earned at the Ruashi mine fed his gambling habit. He wanted to be rich but his wagers and bets drained his money. Determined to recover the losses, he gambled more. He was caught in the web of self-deceit and he eventually dragged both of his children into financing his gambling habit. His destructive impulses were never satisfied.

Where's Daddy? Does he know that Mama is dying? I wonder if he cares?

ఆఆఆ

Esynama reached a familiar road at last, a winding towpath that led to a two-room hut, a wooden structure with boards at odd angles. The roof was made of rusty corrugated iron sections, and the floor was tamped red earth, pounded down by years of footsteps. As she approached her home, she saw the random arrangement of wood and the white curtains wafting in the breeze. Her lovely home was so close it made her heartbeat and legs move faster. She opened the door, and found Moyo holding Mama's hand, keeping vigil.

"How *is* she?" Esynama asked, as she embraced Moyo.

"She's barely breathing."

"Oh, Mama. I love you so!" Esy embraced her mother, holding her tight.

Mama didn't move right away, but slowly lifted her arms to embrace her daughter. "Esy, my sweet girl," she said weakly.

They embraced for a long time, cherishing the moment.

"Has she eaten anything?" Esy asked Moyo, looking directly at him.

"She refuses all the food I offer."

"Let me try," she said. "Mama, I have a delicious piece of banana for you. Please, open your mouth."

Mama moved her head side to side, clenched her teeth and shut her mouth.

"Mama, please."

"No!" she blurted out. "I want to die! I'm in so much pain."

Esy hugged her again and sobbed. "I love you, Mama."

"I have something … for you … under the bed," Mama said weakly.

Esy got on her knees, reached under the bed and found a book. She looked at her mother quizzically.

"You may … open it up."

Esy opened the cover carefully and fifty francs fell out and clattered to the floor. Moyo scrambled to the floor to retrieve them and handed the money to Esy. She turned the pages slowly, seeing they were filled with journal entries and poems. Some of them were cut and pasted on the pages while others were handwritten notes.

"Did you write all of these, Mama?"

"Some ... I wrote for you ... others ... my favorite poets."

"Oh, thank you, Mama! I will keep them close to my heart always." Esy said tearfully, deep down knowing this was her last gift from her mama.

"... Moyo?"

Moyo went to his mother's side. "Yes, Mama."

"I have something ... for my brave son," she said. "There ... in the jar ... on the shelf."

Moyo dashed to the shelf, grabbed the jar and peeked inside. He found fifty francs and a gold chain.

"Thank you, Mama," he said as he ran to hug her.

"These gifts ... from the bottom of my heart. Money is practical ... the gold chain is beautiful ... never forget ... both the practical and the beautiful ... they will make your life happy." Mama was exhausted from all the talk, but she had more to say. "Moyo, work hard... for those you love," her voice trailed off to a whisper. "Come here ... son."

Moyo took her hand and knelt on the floor next to her bed, his face nuzzled sideways just below her shoulder. Esy knelt down on the floor on the other side, put her arm around her mother's waist clutching the journal with her other hand. Esy laid her head on Mama's chest to listen to her heart. She wanted to feel her final breath.

Her breathing stopped well before daylight, but the children kept vigil, holding onto her until the full sun brought in the new day.

Where was Mama now? Will I see her again?

Esy used to listen to her when she told stories about the great man, Simon Kimbangu, who experienced visions from the prophet, Moses. Simon's visions were unforgettable, since they showed him how to heal the Congolese people. Like her mother and the other Kimbanquists, Esy believed in heaven, and she breathed a sigh of relief knowing Mama Mary would be there.

While holding Mama, she heard muffled sounds in the distance. It was the drums, the drums of sorrow, like grief talking. They grew louder and more persistent and, then, she knew Moyo had delivered the message to Daddy Dayana too.

The drumming pierced the warm morning air. "Baboom! Baboom!" Everyone in the radius of eleven kilometers knew that something important had happened. They knew with a certainty that death had visited someone in the night. All the neighbors in the surrounding villages were reminded of the inevitability and presence of death and some of the neighbors drummed back—a message of condolence.

Dayana walked toward the hut and was at the head of the large crowd of people, which grew bigger as they came toward their home. They marched in unison with a purpose. No longer far away, the sound was like booming thunder in Esy's ears. Neighbors, fellow Kimbanquists, the spiritual healers called ngangas, and friends from Elisabethville gathered and grew into a clamorous throng.

Dayana and a neighbor carried their mother's bed outside the hut and placed it under the Baobab tree for all to see. Dayana and the mourners wanted her to have the right burial so she could rest in peace and bless the family from the spirit world. For them, life and death were on a continuum, with death just another state of being. Mary had been transmuted into the spirit world. She had been enfolded into the community of her ancestors and death was considered an exalted state.

The mourners circled around Mary's lifeless body singing, chanting, and crying out. The wailing and grief-cries sent shivers up Esy's spine as they paid their final respects. Stomping feet pounded the red dirt, sending swirls of red, dry dust into the air. The herbs dispersed by the ngangas permeated the air and provided a distinct aura that emanated from the spirit world. The crowd vocalized patterns of loud music as their bodies moved up and down to the rhythm of the drums. Ba-boom, Ba-boom.

Dayana brought three large buckets of rice and mwambe palm oil sauce, manioc roots, and plantains, which he gave to Esy and her mother's closest friend, Fimi. Four men carried a plain hand-carved wooden coffin with a rough-hewn cross on the top, an appropriate emblem of Mary's faith.

Somewhere in between the dancing, wailing and drumming, Dayana collapsed beside Mary's bed and yowled deep, guttural sobs. He shouted prayers and sang driving chants, which seemed to cleanse the air. It was a holy time. This is when Esy understood that Dayana had truly loved her mother. This single action clarified so many confusing thoughts she had about her mother and father.

Finally, the day was spent and the sun settled in the west. It was time to put her mother to rest. Dayana gave one last, soulful cry and then wrapped her mother's body in a shroud, and raised her up high toward the night sky. He looked up and passionately recited *The Lord's Prayer* in Swahili.

Baba Yeta
Baba Yetu uliye mbinguni,
Jina lako litukuzwe;
Ufalme wako ufike,
Utakalo lifanyike
Duniani kama mbinguni,
Utupe leo mkate wetu wa kila siku,
Utusamehe makosa yetu,
Kama nasi tunavyowasamehe waliotukosea.
Usitutie katika kishawishi,
Lakini utuopoe maovuni.
Amina.

He tenderly pulled Mary toward him and held her close for a last embrace.

During the afternoon, Moyo, and some of his neighborhood friends had dug the grave, their duty to show respect for his mother. It was hard work, but shovel full after shovel full they made a large enough hole in the ground for Mary's coffin. Dayana tightened the shroud around Mary's cold body and gently laid her to rest in her coffin, which they placed in the hole underneath the Baobab tree.

Silence fell, the whispers of the people hushed and the drums became still. With hands and shovels, the mourners placed chunks of red earth in the hole to cover Mama's coffin. The chanting resumed. Dayana, Esy and Moyo found one open blossom on the Baobab tree. People in the Congo call this tree "the tree of life."

"It's a sign from heaven," Esy said knowing that most Baobab trees blossom only once a year. Lovingly, they placed the beautiful blossom on the red earth above their mother's grave. She was a Kimbanquist and a blessing to her neighbors.

With her honorable burial complete, it was now time for fire and food. These same neighbors who helped bury Esy's mother built a fire to celebrate the cycle of life with drumming, dancing and singing. The tone was not sad, but accepting of how life goes round and round.

Well-trained by her mother to be a good servant, Esy ran into the house to set out plates, serving dishes, and utensils for the guests. Warm hospitality was a priority for her. With this loving spirit and joy of appreciation, she cultivated the deep connections among her family and friends. Her mother's friend Fimi was helpful and shared the same loving spirit, and both of their actions declared that neighbors are important.

Unlike many others living in the country outside the city, Mama Mary had utensils and dishes for dining in her humble two-room hut. She had received them as wedding gifts from Amelia and Bertrand, her Belgian parents who raised her after she was orphaned as a young girl.

Esy poured the rice, taro and sauce into serving bowls from the buckets of food, while Fimi laid the plantains on the table. It was an abundant banquet so different from their usual fare. They invited the guests to partake of the food. Family and friends streamed into the kitchen to fill their plates. Some took eating utensils and others ate with their hands—either way was accepted. The meal became lively and happy as they squatted and sat around the fire enjoying the rice with mwambe sauce.

With their stomachs full, Mary in her grave, and the burial music finished, the guests lifted their drums and left for home. They had commemorated the cycle of life and the love Mama Mary had for her neighbors and friends.

Now, Esy, Moyo and Dayana were alone and quiet. They went to separate places in the hut. It was time to rest. Esy found the diary that Mama gave her and clutched it close to her chest. She went to her cot along the back wall of the center room behind the worn sofa. Her cot was on the dirt floor and made of woven banana leaves. She could feel the night breezes on her face from the open window above her. She opened her Mama's journal.

Knowing how to read was another gift her mother had given her. She taught Esy all she knew and had learned from Amelia, her Belgian "mother." Amelia had been the head of the household where Mama worked before Esy was born. She had taught school in Belgium when she was younger, and she made sure Mary became educated. Mama said Amelia was a good woman, who went to Mass every day and wanted to make the world a better place. Although her reading wasn't very advanced, Esy could read well enough to understand every word in her mama's journal. There, on the first page, was a poem preceded by a scrawled note that said, *To my dear Esy, this is my favorite poem. Listen to what the writer says. He is a wise man with deep understanding.*

Those Who Are Dead Are Never Gone
By Birago Diop, a Senegalese poet
Those who are dead are never gone:
They are there in the thickening shadow.
The dead are not under the earth:
They are in the tree that rustles,

They are in the wood that groans,
They are in the water that sleeps,
They are in the hut, they are in the crowd,
The dead are not dead.

Those who are dead are never gone,
They are in the breast of the woman,
They are in the child who is wailing
And in the firebrand that flames.
The dead are not under the earth:
They are in the fire that is dying,
They are in the grasses that weep,
They are in the whimpering rocks,
They are in the forest, they are in the house,
The dead are not dead.

Esy walked over to the front window, pulled back the window cloth to the open air, and watched the fire's embers with their dancing orange and red glow. The smoldering remains were mesmerizing. Her ears heard the African wood owl and the whispering sounds of the light breeze on the trees. *It is Mama Mary in the trees. She is the red flickering glow of the subdued fire and the smell of the smoke curling silently into the black night.*

Knowing Mama was not really dead, but her soul lived on, Esy closed the journal, laid it softly on her chest, and fell asleep.

ଔଔଔ

Up with the sun, Dayana, Moyo and Esy met in the kitchen for breakfast. After the manioc root and honey filled their tummies, they smiled at each other knowing that they had done right by Mama Mary. They understood this experience made them grow, not in size, but in wisdom. Walking through and swimming in the river of life made them strong, wise and useful. They belonged to each other and to their community of family and friends.

"Esy, you and I must to go back to the mine," Daddy Dayana said. His voice hardened with his words and his eyes changed and he looked scary to her.

Esy looked down at the floor. She wondered why she couldn't just stay and work in the little house in the country. She could harvest manioc roots, prepare the fruit from the Baobab tree, and express oil from the palm trees. She would be happy doing that work. Going to the mine would make her sad.

Esy recalled the first day at the mine. Daddy Dayana worked for the main boss at the mine did favors for him and organized the work crews. The day he forced Esy to work in the mine with him, she wailed and screamed and hung onto Mama. Daddy Dayana wrestled them apart, grabbed her arm and dragged her along with him. Once there, he released her arm and dropped her with a thud in front of Big Boss. He was the first person she met at the mining camp.

"My, my! What do we have here?" Big Boss said. His large belly jiggled as he laughed. "Quite a beauty, I must say."

That was a new one for Esy because she never considered herself to be a beauty. The thought never crossed her mind. In her fright, she quickly pulled away from his loud strident voice.

"Come here, child," he yelled. "We'll put her in training with Serge for the next couple of weeks," he said to her father.

Big Boss was a big African man with an oppressive stance—arms akimbo. His eyes were dark and piercing—displaying an evil cunning. He had a cavernous wrinkle over the bridge of his crooked nose and his thick lips at rest were set in a permanent frown. Below this face was the body of fat Buddha with lavish rolls of hardened fat cascading from the loose skin of his neck, down his midsection to his groin. By comparison, his legs were skinny—tough and sturdy from carrying the weight of his massive torso. His work "uniform" was always the same—a dirty white short-sleeved shirt with black pants and heavy leather boots.

With that introduction, her days in the camp started. She slept in a three-sided tent on a makeshift mat made of banana leaves. Fruits and fufu, which is dough made from boiled and ground plantain flour, provided by the head cook of the mine minimally sustained her. She learned how to mine cobalt. Esy had a natural aptitude for this hard work. Her eyes spotted the chunks of nickel and copper interwoven with the cobalt, which she picked apart separating the precious bluish gray metal. From sun up to sun down, she worked her fingers until they bled. The sluggish air she breathed worked her lungs hard. Trying to sleep in the heavy air at night made her cough and wheeze.

Big Boss and Daddy Dayana squandered the money from her hard work. At first, Big Boss took all the profits from her and shared only some of it with Daddy Dayana as payment for the work he did. Esy did not get any of the money. After a time, Esy gained their trust and brought her wares directly to the Chinese brokers in Elisabethville, which was the nearest city. The Chinese Brokers would assess the quality of the cobalt she found and exchange the cobalt for francs. Esy gave all the money directly to Daddy Dayana, which meant Big Boss gave him the money for Esy's keep, too. All Esy had to show for her hard work was bruised hands and sliced fingers.

"Daddy, I don't want to go back to the mine."

"But, you must—you are strong and clever," he said. "We need clever hands and eyes to find the cobalt in the water, rocks and slag. Moyo will stay here to harvest and dry the manioc roots, and make palm oil. He is only six and too young to go to the mine."

Reluctantly, Esy put her clothes in a bag and grabbed some plantains for the journey. She wrapped the journal into a soft towel and slipped it into her bag. She knew it would give her hours and hours of good lessons, and she was ready to learn what her mama had to teach her.

Together, Dayana and Esy walked the eight kilometers to the mine. It was a stern, strident walk, like two soldiers going off to war. They did not speak. Even though she dreaded working in the mine, Esy knew what her father said was right. She was proficient at discovering the quality veins of cobalt. She often sieved the mine rocks in muddy pools and streams to find the stones with the purest cobalt content. The other workers would follow her and snaffle her finds, but rather than squabble over the cobalt, she walked around the mine until she found another quality supply.

Ambitious children eked out a living working all day sorting through the rubble of smelted remnants. When finished with their day, they walked two hours to sell their wares to the Chinese brokers. The direct sun was merciless. Even though the brown water on the red earth was invitingly cool in the midday sun, there could be snakes hidden underneath. While Baako, Esy's friend, worked in the brown water, he pulled at something he couldn't see. One tug in the water and a snake hurled its head around, and sank its fangs into Baako's chest. It was a poisonous Naja snake and Baako stopped breathing. Esy's heart was sorrowful and she was scared from that moment on.

In the late afternoon, after working all day, Esy was standing in line at the Chinese Broker's shack when she met an older girl named Asha.

"Do you work in the Ruashi mine?" Esy asked.

"Yes, I've been there for almost a year." Asha replied.

"I've never seen you at the camp. Do you live there?"

"No, I live at the Baptist Mission near here," Asha said. "It's a much better place. The beds are cleaner and the food is very good. I could show you where I live if you want to see it."

"I would like to see it," Esy said smiling. The prospect of finding better living conditions gave Esy some hope. The cobalt dust was making her cough and she yearned for clean air. Asha was taller than Esy with long, skinny legs, but she had an attractive smile. *I think I would like to be her friend.*

She followed Asha to the mission, and was impressed with the missionaries in charge. She asked them if she could stay there.

"We don't have any room right now, but next week Wednesday, one of the rooms will be open," Jackson said. "If you want, I'll save it for you."

"Thank you. I would like that."

After carrying her sack of cobalt to the Chinese broker

at the end of the day on Wednesday, she headed to the mission station in Elisabethville. In another bag she had her clothes and her journal. She appreciated the cleanliness, the food at the mission, and the mattresses. Underneath the mattress was a cot made from woven banana leaves to elevate and cushion the mattress. Still feeling unsure about her surroundings, she hid the money she got from the Chinese vendor under her mattress at night and went to sleep protecting her francs.

Each and every day, Dayana expected her to give him money. That was the only time he acknowledged her at the mine. Outside of that transaction, he never claimed her as his daughter and he seemed harsh and uncaring. She felt lonely and set apart while working at the mine.

Esy's daily grind was the same every day of the week, but in the evening she held her journal tight under her arm. She felt the spirit of Mama Mary—it kept her company through the long, lonely nights.

CHAPTER 2

RAPELAND

 ᘒᘒᘒ

Esy's mama did not work in the Cobalt mines. She instead, lived through the "red rubber era" of Congo's history. Mary worked alongside her mother, tapping and the stinky liquid from the rubber trees. Mother and daughter would trudge through the thick underbrush with pails in hand. Mary's mother had an eye for the trees that would produce the most latex. The trees had to be about six years old and at least six inches in diameter. Once she spotted a good prospect, she would expertly slice a quarter-inch deep groove into the bark with her hooked knife. This quick, decisive stroke took skill and practice. Then, she would peel back the bark about twelve inches and a milky white substance would quickly flow out and follow the downward spiraling of the fresh cut groove and spill into the pail.

Doing this work early in the morning was always the best, because once the temperature started to rise, the liquid would coagulate and seal the cut. Mary's goal was to get the most latex into the pail before this would happen. The liquid rubber would collect in the pails for five hours and then Mary's mother would tap the other side of the tree, so the fresh cut on the previous side could heal.

All day they would tap the rubber trees doing several at a time. Before noon one day, three sentries filed through the forest, checking on the rubber harvest. Thinking Mary's mother was alone in the forest, they challenged her in a loud voice. Mary hid behind a tree and peered around to see if her mama was okay. She saw them drag her through the weeds to rape her. Hearing her mother scream, she froze with fright. Her heart pounded against her heart so hard, she passed out. The perpetrators never knew she was lying in the tall weeds by the rubber trees. With laughter, and a yowling, the three sentries left the way they came.

She stayed hidden in the grass for a very long time. The heat of the midday sun beat down on her body. Later that afternoon, another sentry with a different colored skin tromped through the woods and spotted Mary in the weeds. He asked her gently if her mother was the woman he had found beaten further down the row of rubber trees. Seized by terror, Mary's heart was beating so fast she couldn't speak. She nodded a quick yes, and the man scooped her off the ground and carried her away under his arm—like a piece of lumber. Her only view was of the sentry's legs moving back and forth as he tromped through the rubber forest.

The man's legs were whiter than hers and hairy. He wore tan shorts and leather shoes that kicked the under-brush away. As they left the forest, the air smelled so much better than the rubber stench. The sun shone with fuller, more radiant light. They had left the forest behind with its overarching canopy of rubber trees. The sentry looked down and saw her eyes open and alert. When he moved her from under his arm to the crook of his arm like how her daddy used to carry her when she was little, Mary was not afraid.

New sights filled her eyes with overflowing wonder. Everything seemed whiter and cleaner. The houses were delicately pastel, or white, with fences and bright flowers. The trees lining the streets were all the same size, their evenness matched. The roads were hard and dust free, filled with bicycles, carriages and other moving vehicles that made a sputtering sound. No more putrid, rubber smells, no more sickening, open sewer smells, which was pervasive in the little village where she was born.

The man suddenly placed her firmly on the ground and told her to hold his hand. With firm resolve, he walked up to one of the lovely houses and knocked on the door. A beautiful lady answered. She was wearing a long white gown with a high collar. Her hair was light brown, fastened in the back with a gentle upsweep. Her eyes were clear blue and her lips formed a delicate smile.

"Madam Amelia," the sentry said, "Bertrand asked me to find a servant girl to help you around the house, and I found this little girl for you. Her mother was killed this morning, so she needs someone to take care of her. Watch out 'cause she passes out when she's afraid. She seems to be a nice little girl, though, so I hope she works out."

With that said, he turned around and left.

Mary stood motionless, staring at the lady in the white

dress with the lace collar. Madam Amelia looked mostly amused and radiated sweetness.

"What's your name?" she asked, motioning to make sure the little girl understood.

"Mary," the little frightened girl responded.

From that inauspicious beginning, Mary's life as a servant girl turned out to be a stroke of good fortune. Amelia was a teacher, and she took Mary on as her next project. Mary was in Elisabethville, a Belgian enclave in the Katanga region of the Congo.

Bertrand, Amelia's husband, was an engineer who worked for a copper and cobalt mine in the Katanga Province, so he was often away for long stretches at a time. Mary and Amelia became attached to one another and acted almost like buddies. Living in Africa separated Amelia from all she had known in England and Belgium, and Mary, a young orphan, soon latched onto her. Mary was a bright student in all areas and she learned how to clean, cook and—most valuable of all—she learned how to speak English and French.

For Amelia, it was the unfolding of a dream. She had acquired a student, a servant and a companion. This was the best way to stave off the loneliness that came from being so far from home and with her husband away so much of the time. For ten years, the relationship filled the needs for both of them. Bertrand spent most of his time working at the mines as an engineer in a consulting capacity. He enjoyed the esprit de corps of working with men and he really didn't understand his wife. Mary mitigated the estrangement they felt in their marriage, and Bertrand referred to Amelia and Mary as a "match made in heaven."

Mary tried in vain for years to make her hair look like Amelia's. She wanted her soft white skin and blue eyes, but when she looked in the mirror, dark skin, brown eyes and frizzy hair stared back at her. Deep down, she knew she didn't belong in Amelia's world. By all appearances, the relationship between Amelia and Mary seemed to be a smooth relationship until puberty reared its ugly head.

A restlessness rose within Mary as the need to discover herself grew. She wanted to find out about her people and she began a desperate search for her origins. In her teen years, many questions about her mother and father surfaced. When she asked people about her family, they gave her blank stares. She was nobody from nowhere. Those unrelenting feelings motivated her to get answers and understand her African roots.

After dark, when the work in the mines was finished, a group of laborers hit the nightlife in Elisabethville. The bar they frequented was close to where Mary lived. They were an easy bunch, fun loving and a bit cocky. There was one young man by the name of Dayana who caught her eye. She liked the serious side of him, which he showed just once in a while. He was different from the others. The others just wanted to have a good time.

She planned her evening walks at about the time the sun was setting, so she could watch the miners from the other side of the street as they were going to the bar. Of course, Amelia gave her many warnings not to mingle with those kind of boys. Amelia considered behavior like that to be unsuitable for a young lady, especially for someone who had been educated in the finer things of life. But, Mary's curiosity got the better of her.

She gave Mary lessons on how to behave and other

lessons in literature, history, math, and two different languages. Mary could read and speak fluently in both English and French. It was unfortunate, but this knowledge set her apart from her peers so most of the time she was either by herself, or with Amelia. She had trouble finding close friends. Mary was African on the outside but European on the inside.

Mary always tried to listen to the men talking when she saw Dayana go to the bar. He was passionate, and humorously opinionated. Once, Mary overheard him arguing about religion with one of the other miners. It was a vigorous debate, because Mary could hear their argument from the other side of the street. She heard the word Kimbanquist over and over again. *What was that?* Driven to find out, the next night, at sundown, she walked across the street, sidled up to Dayana and introduced herself. Surprised by her advances, Dayana hesitated to give her his name and just stared at her. She returned his stare, and he finally blurted out, "Dayana."

"What is Kimbanquist?" Mary asked, continuing to stare at him until he answered.

"Why would a girl want to know about Kimbanquist?" He said in Swahili while stifling a laugh.

"I like big words and I am curious," she responded in Swahili.

At that point in time, Dayana showed his serious side and spent over an hour sharing all he knew about Simon Kimbangu. Because he grew up in a church that was run by Baptist missionaries, Dayana shared Simon's strong Christian belief and value system. He went on to mention that Simon demonstrated many acts of healing through faith. Dayana relayed the story about receiving visions from Moses and how he needed to heal the Congolese people.

Most important, Dayana told Mary about his strong anti-European sentiment, which made him value the traditional African religions. His ideas of religion made Mary's ears perk up, because at this time in her life she felt like an interloper, bogged down by the European influences in her life. She yearned to break away and become free.

Mary was searching for a religion that would elevate her African roots. Maybe becoming a Kimbanguist was the answer. Simon Kimbangu incorporated traditional African beliefs with his Christian beliefs, which taught that spirits inhabit objects so God can be found in a tree, a rock, the ocean, or any other natural force. He stressed the belief that God is all around and in everything.

CRCRCR

When Esy was a child, Mama Mary talked about the Kimbanquists. Mama Mary emphasized they believed in Christ, and that many of his beliefs were "anti-European." Simon fused Christianity with traditional African religions. He had a dislike for European religious traditions and especially disliked the use of European names for the precious African children. One day, when Mama Mary and Esy were cooking together, her mama demonstrated how the Kimbanquists blended the two religions by stirring manioc root and curry together to make a different color combination.

"See, Esy? That's how Simon did it," Mama said. "I gave you and your brother African names to remind you of your African roots. It is a precious heritage."

The Kimbanquists showed Mama how to be a proud African. Mama always regretted having the name "Mary." She didn't fit with her African friends because of her name. Daddy Dayana agreed with Mama's desire to get back to the African roots, so he took her away from Amelia and Bertrand and their European influence to live in the country outside of Elisabethville. Daddy and Mama made sure their children had African names.

ରେ ରେ ରେ

During their courtship, the more Dayana talked, the more his comments resonated with Mary. Another part of this religion Mary liked was it rejected violence, polygamy, witchcraft, alcohol and tobacco. Mary's mother had suffered a violent death at the hands of the brutal sentries and she could hear her mother's screams in her dreams. The wicked laughter of the sentries as they repeatedly tortured her became an endless nightmare.

Mary's hatred of brutality to control people ran deep. She began to respect Dayana's views of abstaining from forcefully harming another person. Emboldened by Mary's respect and adulation, Dayana found the courage to ask her to go to church with him that following Sunday. She feared that Amelia would be upset with such behavior, so Mary hesitated to give him an answer. Finally, Mary assured Dayana that she would give him an answer by sundown the next day.

"I have something to ask," Mary said as she approached Amelia. "I have met someone who is a Kimbanquist."

"You have?"

"Yes, and he asked me to go to church with him."

"I know about the Kimbanquists. They are good

people," Amelia said. "I've always wondered why it's against their religion to wear shoes."

"Maybe it has something to do with being African."

"Maybe."

"Could I go to church with him this Sunday?"

"Is he a nice boy?" Amelia asked.

"Yes, very nice."

"Okay, but be on your best behavior. Don't forget what I've taught you."

"I'll remember."

That was how it started. In only a two years time, Mary and Dayana became Kimbanquists and were married. They had two children, a girl and a boy and they gave them African names, Esynama and Moyo.

ෲෲෲ

The day in the mine was over and the sun had set. Esy sold her cobalt at the market and headed toward the mission to find her space to sleep for the night. It was quiet now but she knew that the sun would soon rise to greet a new workday. Tonight she had a strong urge to read her mother's journal.

The last time she looked at those pages, she read the poem by Birago Diop, *Those Who are Dead are Never Gone*. It helped her understand the "life" of the dead. She opened the next page and read the journal entry.

My Dear Esy,

This is a story about names and where you came from. When Dayana and I were married we wanted you and Moyo to love Africa, your homeland. My mama gave me the name of Mary to remind me of her sister, but I always wanted another name, an African name. You and your brother have African names because they are beautiful names and because they will remind you of where you belong. Moyo means "with heart" and Esy or Esynama means "God hears you," so pray to God and you can be assured that he will answer your prayers. He will listen to you and take care of you.

I love you,

Mama Mary

Those words reassured her. She felt a peaceful calm knowing that God would protect her. Esy placed the journal under her bed of banana leaves and fell into a deep sleep.

Upon waking she breathed in the warm clean air. As she recalled the diary entry, she reveled in the deep love her mama had for her. Even when she was sick, Mama loved her children the best way she could and remained caring to the very end. With renewed confidence, Esy washed, dressed, ate some manioc root and honey for breakfast as was her custom. She grabbed a couple of plantains to sustain her through the day.

Her friend Asha slept in the room down the hall in the mission. Esy tried to share a room with her, but it just didn't work. Asha snorted and yelled out names during the night. She was always yelling and scolding someone in her dreams. Esy would wake her and tell her to stop, but it was like talking to a wooden log. In the morning Asha had no recollection of her dreams and would giggle about the stories Esy would tell. Asha had a busy nightlife. One story she told amused Esy. She had heard Asha in a scolding tone yell "Dabuka, Dabuka" then she mumbled curt snorts, wagged her finger and said "sleep with one eye open because I'm going to tell on you." Esy later discover that Dabuka was her little brother and a troublemaker.

Fortunately, the missionary couple in charge found another room for Esy. Despite the fact that they didn't share a room, Asha and Esy were a team when walking to and from the mine. They shared their food, flirted with the boys as they worked, and talked about their families. Asha had a mama but no daddy and Esy had a daddy but no mama, so they had supported each other while working at the mine.

Children as young as six years old and as old as fifteen trickled out of the huts along the way heading to the Ruashi mine. They assembled in groups of threes and fours shouting greetings and teasing each other. Coughing from the pernicious fumes was inevitable and yet, no one in charge seemed concerned about how destructive the fumes were to the children's health. The children put up with it because, unfortunately, this was the only way they could earn money in the Congo. They didn't earn much, though, because Big Boss seized most of the money. They tried to lighten their hard work with occasional laughter to keep them going.

Separating the sharp cobalt from the copper and nickel left the children's fingers and hands cut and bruised. In some cases they could use a pickaxe, but much of the cobalt was in remnants from the smelting process, called slags, which were found in the contaminated water pools in the mine. At the end of a very long workday, the children still had to carry their full sacks of cobalt to Elisabethville, which was a two and one half hour walk. The

Chinese market was always waiting to gobble up their day's work for a few francs. These brokers had an insatiable appetite for this precious metal. Once they paid for the cobalt, they sent it to China for further refinement. They made three hundred to four hundred percent profit from the hard work of the children.

CRCRCR

One morning, to everyone's surprise, Big Boss was standing on the edge of the hill watching the children file past. He silently glared down at them. Messing with him was like stirring up a hornet's nest. The smart ones kept their distance. As Esy walked past, she could feel his eyes follow her. Her hair stood on end and clung to her friend Asha for safety. She thought that going directly to the scrap hill on the far side of the mine might get her away from Big Boss's gaze. Asha sensed Esy's unease, so she followed her into the same work area.

With Asha beside her, the day of mining was a productive one for Esy. She harvested a bag full of cobalt and was eager to have it weighed and assessed by the Chinese broker. She knew it was quality cobalt. At sunset, Asha and Esy left the mine and walked together to the market to sell their cobalt. She was pleased to see that she did get more francs than usual.

On the way back to the mission station to settle in for the night, they heard quick but heavy footsteps behind them. Panicked, they turned around to see the specter of Big Boss coming toward them. When he was about to catch up with them, Asha and Esy took off running.

Big Boss called out from behind them, "Don't be afraid. I have a favor to ask of Esy."

Esy turned and stood still, but her mind was still in flight mode ready at a moment's notice to leap into the bushes and run away from him.

"Dayana told me that you understand English," he panted, out of breath after trying to catch up with them.

Esy nodded.

"I received a letter from America and I don't know what it says. I think it's about purchasing Cobalt directly from us, but I'm not sure. Would you be able to translate it for me?"

Speechless with surprise, Esy nodded.

"Come to my shack at the mine first thing in the morning."

Once again Esy hesitated before responding with a nod. Mystified as to why Big Boss needed her to translate, Esy's curiosity was greater than being alarmed by his sudden affability. She tried to keep an open mind and stay alert to anything that might be suspicious. He was scary, but Daddy Dayana seemed to trust him, so maybe he was okay.

It was a long, hard day, and Esy looked forward to dinner, reading Mama's journal, and having a good night's sleep. The simple meal at the Baptist mission house was nourishing. It consisted of saka saka, also known as cassava leaf soup, palm oil and salt fish and sometimes, they served fufu. Asha and Esy ate their fill and went to their rooms for some quiet time before bed. Esy couldn't wait to read more of her mother's journal. Each entry was like a new discovery, a special treasure.

Dear Esy,

I want to tell you about Amelia and Bertrand. They contributed so much to my life. For ten years, Amelia was like a mother to me. She introduced me to so many different worlds. I learned math, literature, social studies, history, French, and English. We laughed often and helped each other. Bertrand was never home much, but when he was he took us along on trips. Amelia and I prepared the food, packed the picnic basket, and we drove to the beautiful Lake Mweru, which is part of Rift Valley.

Esy, please try to find a way to get an education. Amelia opened so many new worlds for me, and it adds so much to life to learn about God's world. It will help you, your children, and the next generation.

Bertrand and Amelia lived in a lovely home at 100 Ave des Sapiniers. They had wonderful neighbors near by and a very friendly church. Amelia went to Mass everyday and I often went with her. At Christmas time, we decorated the house with red, green and white ornaments and beautiful Crèches. I loved Amelia very much and she loved me, a humble orphan. She was a good Mom. I hope you can meet someone like Amelia when you need help and are ready for a new experience.

I love you always,

Mama Mary

Her mama's words gave Esy peace, helped her create dreams, and gave her comfort. All of this helped her sleep peacefully. The journal filled her cup to overflowing. She was ready to go to bed, but there was one question on her mind: *What will happen tomorrow with Big Boss?*

CHAPTER 3

Hackett Salomon

ଔଔଔ

Where wilt thou find a cavern dark enough
To mask thy monstrous visage? Seek none, conspiracy:
Hide it in smiles and affability.
Julius Caesar, William Shakespeare

Big Boss was polite as Esy entered the open door of his shed. He appeared cheerful and greeted her in a fine, gentlemanly way. He asked her if she would like a glass of mango. Esy nodded and he gave her a chilled glass of juice, while encouraging her to have a seat. His unexpected generosity dumbfounded her, but she soon became comfortable with this princess-like treatment, choosing to become less wary. He expressed appreciation of her good work at the mine and praised the hard work of her daddy, Dayana. He asked her how old she was and, when Esy said eleven, he seemed surprised that such a young lady could be so knowledgeable and literate. Big Boss was complimentary, and it seemed genuine. His crooked nose was unsightly, but his large smile welcomed and warmed her.

He showed Esy the letter from the United States, gave her some quiet time to read it and translate it into Swahili. She tried to make an accurate and clear translation for Big Boss by summarizing the letter.

"A weapons company in Pittsburgh wants to purchase unrefined cobalt directly from your mine before the Chinese brokers send it to their country for refining. They are asking you to respond by letter to inform them if this is a possibility."

With that said, Esy pointed to the address written in the last paragraph and let Big Boss know where to send his response. When finished with the translation, she looked at Big Boss to determine if he wanted more from her. His smile and nod of approval told her she had satisfied him. He complimented her ability to translate and then, out of the blue, asked her if she saw Daddy Dayana while working at the mine. She informed him that she saw him only in the morning when he collected the francs from her for the previous day's work. He nodded, smiled and seemed pleased by that answer. After a slight pause, he asked her to stop by before work the next day. Esy nodded and left.

When she was behind the mining piles and out of sight of Big Boss, Esy ran as fast as she could to find Asha, and found her working by herself in the area that Esy discovered was filled with high quality cobalt. She embraced her friend, hoping to shake off the anxiety that had settled in her stomach. Confused by the sudden burst of emotion, Asha asked her what had happened. Esy calmed down and told her the whole story. They both wondered why Big Boss wanted her to come to his shed the next day. They shrugged and continued looking for the cobalt among the piles of slag. Concentrating on her work was difficult, and Esy did not fill her bag, which was unlike her. That meant she didn't get as many francs from the Chinese market for Daddy Dayana.

Esy and Asha's agitation made them restless so they played two-man soccer until they were limp with exhaustion. As was their plan, their fatigue helped them sleep despite the worry about the next day,

The next morning Esy persuaded Asha to come with her to the shed. Big Boss was waiting by the door. With ceremony and a gracious smile, he greeted them. He offered each of them a glass of chilled mango juice. The first tasty swallow lit up their faces with smiles, and Big Boss chuckled. He complimented Asha on her diligent work in the mine and with a casual wave requested her to leave so he could speak to Esy alone. He waited a few minutes for Asha to shut the door behind her, and then Big Boss made some comments about her translation of the letter, asking her how she learned to read English. Esy looked at him quizzically, wondering why he wanted to know, but she explained to him that a Belgian school-teacher taught her mother, and in turn, Mama Mary tutored her.

Big Boss paused, scrutinized Esy's face and then, smiled as he pointed to a diploma from Université Catholique, conferring a Bachelor's Degree in Engineering on Hackett Salomon. Esy didn't understand. He proceeded to give her a long lecture about his exploits as a young man while a college student in Belgium. As she listened to his

self-aggrandizement, a wide-eyed and gullible Esy inno-
cently asked, "Who is Hackett Salomon?"

"I'm Hackett Salomon," his indignation plain. When
Esy said nothing in response, Hackett waited for her adulation, but it never came. He paused for a moment then
changed the direction of his monologue. "I think you
would do very well studying at the university."

This surprised Esy's. *Could this be the opportunity I've
been waiting for? Hackett Salomon has experienced education, and he could show me the way out of the mine and into
the classroom.*

He offered her some of his old textbooks to read. Flab-
bergasted by his generosity, Esy thanked him, cradled the
books in her arms, and turned to leave the shed to start
her day's work in the mine. Before she passed through
the door, Hackett asked her to return the textbooks to
him after she read them. She nodded and then, went in
search of her friend Asha. But, Asha wasn't where Esy
expected her to be, so she went to work by herself. As
she was looking for cobalt in the smelted dregs, thoughts
raced through her mind. *I am so excited about going to
school to become educated. Once I forge a path to education,
I can help Moyo, my brothers go to school. Mama would be
so proud of me.*

Esy returned to her mining work with renewed focus.
She hurried to take her bag to the Chinese market to
exchange cobalt for francs. She cut the usual two to
three-hour walk to a little over two hours, so she would
have something to give to Daddy Dayana the next morning. The biggest advantage of living at the mission station
was not having to make the trip back to the mine after a
long workday.

After selling her cobalt, Esy was eager to get to the mission and talk with Asha about the events of the day. She stood by Asha's bedroom door about to enter when she heard her friend sobbing. Esy tapped on the door and opened it a crack. Asha, with tears flowing, rushed into her arms. Esy looked at her lovingly and waited for her to share what was happening.

"Big Boss is sending me to a mine on the other side of Elisabethville, so I won't be able to work with you anymore," Asha blurted out. "He said they need someone talented like me to find cobalt in the other mine. I will have to find another place to sleep at night because it's just too far to walk here after working all day."

"I will miss you so much," Esy said. "You are a good friend." They held each other for a long time. Esy felt a wave of loneliness wash over her knowing that her one and only true friend would be far away. From now on, working at the mine would be lonely and isolating.

Esy shook her head as she walked back to her room. *Why did Big Boss do that? Sometimes he would move the boys around, but never the girls. Maybe I'll ask him why when I return the books.*

She placed Hackett's textbooks on her bed and carefully paged through each one. The textbook on World Literature was written in French, and the other on Geology was written in English. She had a basic knowledge of both languages, but it would take her time to read the books. She looked in the index to find Birago Diop in the World Literature textbook. The section on Africa contained an entry for Birago Diop for his book, *Tales of Amadou Kaumba,* but she didn't see her favorite poem.

Instead, she decided she would try to find *Tales of Amadou Kaumba* somewhere, since she enjoyed his work.

The geology textbook was fascinating too. She looked up cobalt and discovered things she hadn't known about the metal. Her fingers could identify cobalt with her eyes closed, but she didn't understand why the metal was so prized. The Germans called cobalt "Kobold," which meant "demon" in their language. Cobalt was used in weapons, and it gave off a strange glow so she could understand why they would give it such a name. Also, it has unusual properties, such as a high melting point and the ability to remain strong at high temperatures, and it seemed impervious to air and water. She read that it remained stable during explosions. Even acids had only minimal corrosive effect on this unique metal. Apparently, this made the metal useful for machinery and weapons. Once the captains of industry and military engineers had discovered the strength of this metal, Cobalt was in high demand.

Hackett Salomon's act of generosity in sharing his textbooks sparked within Esy an insatiable desire to learn. Her mother was right when she wrote in her journal that education opens up new worlds. Esy made a list of questions to ask Hackett about his experience in education.

Within the week, she had read the textbooks, made a list of questions, and was ready to confer with Hackett on her way to work in the morning. As she approached his shed, he opened the door. Esy greeted him with respect.

"Good morning, Mr. Salomon."

"You may call me Hackett," he responded with an ingratiating smile. "Did you enjoy reading the textbooks?"

"I learned so much," Esy said. "I enjoyed learning about cobalt and my favorite writer, Birago Diop."

"Well, well. He's my favorite too," Hackett replied. "We have so much in common. Do you think you might be interested in going to the university?"

"Yes, very much."

"I know a gentleman that might be able to help you with that," Hackett said, as he handed her a piece of paper with his address. "He lives in Elisabethville just a few blocks inside the city. His name is Viktor von Peeters. He would like to talk to you."

"When will I meet him?" Esy asked.

"Tomorrow afternoon, around two."

"Thank you. I'll plan to meet him then," Esy said eagerly. She so wanted her dream of education to come true. *I think this is what I've been waiting for. I can't wait to meet Viktor von Peeters.*

০৪০৪০৪

The next morning, Esy woke up, put on the better of her two dresses, grabbed a black plantain, and headed east toward Elisabethville. Since Esy was a Kimbanquist, she did not wear shoes. Looking down at her bare feet, she was certain they would be dirty and dusty by the time she met Mr. von Peeters, but hoped she would still make a good enough impression. Mr. von Peeters was an educated man, so Hackett Solomon had said. She wanted make a good impression and be clean, neat and respectable. Esy retrieved the slip of paper Hackett Salomon gave to her and read, "3 Congo Street." Congo Street was a major thoroughfare, so Esy was confident she could find it. Her spirits were high with hope that this could be the big break she was waiting for. Going to school and becoming educated held so much promise. It could change her life forever.

As she approached the address, she saw a neat white clapboard house offset by purple Lobelia bushes. Esy put her face close expecting the pretty flower to have a lovely smell, but instead it was disgusting. She pulled away from the odor, stood up, and knocked on the door. She waited, but nobody came. She knocked again and finally, the door opened. A tall, slender blonde man gestured her to come inside. Esy stood in the foyer waiting for directions about what to do next. He said nothing—just stood there mute. Only his eyes moved. He scanned her up and down several times. Esy's stomach became queasy as she found herself caught between wanting to make a good impression and wanting to run away and hide. *Why doesn't he say something to me? Is there something wrong with me? What should I do?*

"Well, miss. I would like you to meet some of my friends," he said with his eyes half shut, looking slick as a fox. "They'll be here next week, come back then."

"Will they help me get educated?" Esy asked.

"Yes, they are very nice, and they will help you get educated."

"Okay, I will come," she said. As she turned, she tried to see his eyes one more time, but he quickly shut the door behind her.

What was that all about? I think he's a scary, mean man. I'm not sure I want to go back. On her walk, Esy pondered what she should do and wished she had someone to talk to. Feeling alone and isolated, she thought about her friend Asha. She didn't have to go back to the mine that day, so visiting her at the mission might be just what she needed.

Esy recalled a map on the wall showing other Baptist outposts in the area, the one where Asha stayed was about four kilometers away. She hoped she could make it before it was too late for dinner. As she walked by other mining operations, she noticed how the industry had chewed-up the environment. Piles of sand, gravel and red dirt sprung up like carbuncles on the land. Acrid smells of refineries and smelting ores permeated the air. The mining companies had waste products of the extracted metals scattered everywhere with no rhyme or reason. What an ugly mess! This chaotic landscape fueled her dream for an education—she wanted to get away from this ugliness.

Her fast pace paid off as she arrived at the mission just when the dinner of salt fish and cassava bread, one of her favorite meals, was being served. Esy was so famished that she filled her plate even before she looked around for Asha. As she stuffed food in her mouth, someone came up behind her and covered her eyes and started to giggle. Esy knew immediately it was her funny friend, Asha, but she played along.

"Guess who?" Asha asked. Keeping Esy's eyes covered, she demanded answers to some questions. "What is my favorite color?"

"Is it yellow?" Esy asked.

"No."

"Is it black?"

"No! No!" was the reply.

"I know. It's purple," Esy exclaimed.

Hearing the lively banter, the other children, the adults and the cooks gravitated to the fun by clapping and joining in the laughter. The adults asked Asha if Esy was her sister and she giggled with delight as she told them she was her good friend from the Ruashi mine. She explained they met each other at that mine.

"Could I stay the night with you?" Esy pleaded.

"I need to ask the missionaries, Mary Ann and David," Asha responded.

Hardly a moment passed before Mary Ann came to Esy, welcoming her to the mission station. She gave Esy a warm hug. So relieved by her generosity, Esy hugged her back. Mary Ann took her hand and walked her to the office to meet her husband, David. He responded to the introductions with a genuine smile, shook her hand, and asked a few questions about herself. Sensing that he was trustworthy, Esy described in detail about her encounters with Hackett Salomon and his friend Viktor von Peeters. She mentioned how she had translated a letter for Hackett and told David he promised to help her get an education.

David's face turned glum and serious as she shared the rest of her story.

"Esy, you must be careful with those men. They might have other plans besides helping you go to school."

Esy sobered and listened to his weighty remarks. She understood what he was saying was very important.

"There is an extra bed in Asha's room for you," he said. "You can stay the night here."

"Thank you, David."

The two friends were so happy to see each other. Their infectious laughter attracted groups of children as they played outside after supper. They held hands as they walked down the hallway to their room. Esy and Asha talked well into the night about what they were doing and the people they met. Asha questioned the promises Big Boss and Viktor von Peeters made about educating her. She hoped, for Esy's sake, they really meant it. The excitement of seeing each other again exhausted them. As their bodies fell into bed, they yielded to a deep sleep. In the middle of the night, Esy woke up suddenly when she heard Asha make loud snorts and utter angry words.

"Dabuka. Dabuka!" Asha chided. "You better sleep with one eye open because I'm going to get you!"

Once Esy was aware of where she was, she broke into laughter. Asha, her funny friend, hadn't changed a bit. Knowing she had to get up at the crack of dawn, Esy tried hard to get back to sleep. Daylight came too soon, but after she took time to do her usual yawning and stretching, she put on her dress, grabbed a couple of plantains from the kitchen, and started on the long journey back to the mine. She would see Asha again in a week.

ക്കക്ക

"There is a game of April Fool that's played behind its door,
Where the fool remains forever and the April comes no more,
Where the splendor of the daylight grows drearier than the dark,
And life droops like a vulture that once was the Blue Bird;
For the Devil is a gentleman, and doesn't keep his word."
G.K. Chesterton

Esy always worked hard at the mine to make money for Daddy Dayana, but her trips to Elisabethville meant less time to do that work. Daddy Dayana was disappointed she had fewer francs at the end of the week and he didn't hide his displeasure. Esy eyes averted his and her head hung low. But she wasn't really sorry. The desire she had for education was stronger than her desire to make money.

Today was the day she would meet the friends of Viktor von Peeters. She tidied up the best she could and took a couple of plantains for her journey. Her heart swelled just thinking about the possibility of attending school. This might be the turning point of her life, so she remained hopeful.

The dusty roads were bedeviled with large stones and ruts, slowing her travel time. The arduous journey tormented her body. Her legs ached and her feet were sore from the stones on the road. The landscape was unusually arid this time of year with meager crops of millet along the roadway. The dry red dirt gusted up like whirls of smoke puffs. The closer she came to the little white house with the Lobelia flowers, the queasier her stomach. They looked good, but smelled bad. At one point she stopped, looked up in the sky and uttered a prayer for courage. She kept moving forward, but in her mind's eye, she saw the image of David's scowling face when she told him about Mr. von Peeters. She was overwhelmed with fear, felt helpless and all alone against the world. Her thoughts turned dark and scary.

A loud male voice jarred her out of her daze. Coming out through the open windows of the little white house were rowdy guffaws—men talking and laughing. One of them peered out the window and spotted her walking up to the front door.

"She's here," he shouted. "The little black girl is here." The other two men responded with a sporting laugh. Esy's heart pounded hard—*what should I do?* Horrified and paralyzed by their taunts, she started to cry. Temporarily immobilized, she still could hear them scramble to the front of the house, and Esy panicked.

She heard the door creak open and decided all at once to turn tail and run. With tears of fright in her eyes, she loped like a gazelle down the road and away from the house. Their uncouth behavior didn't square with her understanding of how nice, educated people would act.

"Go after her," Viktor shouted an order to the youngest one. The chosen one charged out of the door at a fast clip.

Esy ran as fast as she could diving down streets and turning sharp corners. Suddenly, she found herself in an alley, looking at the backs of houses. Heavy footfalls pounded behind her. She risked a glance and saw a man with long strides gaining on her. She tried to pick up her pace, but he was getting closer. *What should I do? I can't run as fast as he can. He has longer legs, so I have to be smarter and cleverer.* Maybe it was the games of soccer that gave her the understanding she had to find another strategy besides speed to win. It was imperative that she hide until he stopped the chase. She darted around one house and then another, leading him on a wild chase. Behind the third house, she found a burn barrel on its side. *I could just fit inside of that barrel.* The smell was sickening and the barrel was half full of cold ash, but she crawled inside and covered herself up with the ash. There was no top on barrel, so she curled up at the bottom of the barrel to be out of sight. She waited quietly. She heard the man's footsteps as he darted around the house. They stopped and Esy hoped he would give up. When he started up again he walked slowly, his steps dwindling to a creep. She could hear the scuff of his shoes on the dusty path—so frighteningly close. Jarred by an angry kick on the barrel, Esy wanted to cry out, but collected herself and stayed as steady as a rock. Esy didn't breathe or move a single muscle. The man scraped his shoe on the side of the barrel as he turned around to leave. She listened intently as his footfalls became fainter and fainter and then finally, stop ...

CHAPTER 4

Running To...

ႣႽჁႽჁႽ

Esy stayed curled up in that stinky burn barrel for a long time. Dusk came and she heard the family in the nearby house come home for supper. When she was confident Viktor's henchman had stopped his search, she cleared a path inside the barrel so she could breathe cleaner air.

Esy spent time deep in thought about her life. Daddy Dayana didn't care about her, he just wanted money for his gambling life. Hackett Salomon didn't care. His promises were false and he was a debauched lecher. Viktor von Peeters didn't care, he wanted to exploit her—he had francs in his eyes. David's warning was real and she sensed evil hearts in these men. Esy reckoned she would have to strike out on her own, find her way to an education, and once she succeeded, she would make sure her little brother Moyo had better opportunities.

She waited until the house was dark and the family

off to bed before she climbed out of the barrel. First, she brushed herself off. Her legs were stiff, and her body smelled like she had been roasted. Three bright spots in her life were Maryann, David, and Asha. With them on her mind, she ran to the nearby mission station.

The moon was brilliant and full. It shone on her path and helped light the way. She traveled to the other side of Elisabethville to get to the mission station. Esy's eyes scanned the bushes for any shadows of her chaser... or maybe there were more than one chasing her. She didn't see anyone, but her eyes stayed alert. She kept a steady running pace moving toward her destination. At the outskirts of Elisabethville, a party was going on at the bar. She was afraid to draw attention to herself after what had happened earlier, so she tiptoed behind the bushes to stay out of sight as she moved beyond the party.

With about one kilometer left to get to the mission station, Esy proceeded with renewed caution hoping to remain invisible. As she walked through the bushes, however, she accidently rustled up a nest of bush babies, tiny nocturnal monkeys that lived in the forest. Esy was spooked. Hearing the rustling and snapping of the branches from their mad scamper, she looked up and saw multiple eyes glowing, piercing the dark like eerie beams from another world. The family of small monkeys bolted higher in the trees and cried like babies. The loud cries and the rapid swinging between the trees thwarted her effort to glide through the bushes undetected. To her relief, however, nobody noticed, and she continued her journey.

She arrived at the mission station in the middle of the night when all were sound asleep. Not wanting to wake anyone up, Esy curled up in a chair on the porch. Her exhausted body finally relaxed and she slept. Many of the children—including Asha—worked in the Etoile mine, and their workday began at the crack of dawn. As Asha left for the mine, she opened the screen door and gasped when she found Esy curled up in the chair.

"Esy, Esy!" she said, shaking her. "Are you okay?" Asha touched her dirty arms dangling out of the chair. "What is all over your body?

Esy recognized her friend's voice, opened her eyes and smiled, "Hi, Asha," she said. "Yes, I'm fine."

Asha shook her head as she listened to Esy's account of her harrowing tale. When Esy finished, Asha hugged her friend, so relieved she was alive.

"What will you do now?" Asha asked. " You know, Esy, those men are evil. They want to use you—and education isn't part of their plan."

"David said the same thing, so I have decided to venture out on my own, but something keeps calling me back to the mission at the Ruashi mine." Esy said with her head bowed.

"What?" she asked. "Why would you want to go back there?"

"The journal Mama Mary gave me is still under my bed there, I *have* to get it. I *must* go back, I must. I have to get it."

"You can sleep in my bed *after* you bathe," Asha declared. "I'll finish up at the mine early today so you and I can walk together to get your journal. That way you'll be safer."

"Thank you, thank you."

Esy went to the mission office to talk to David only

to find a note on his door that said he would be out all morning. Esy washed her hands and face, took off her dress and washed the ash out of it, and placed it on the sill to dry in the sun. After that, she nestled into her friend's bed and fell asleep.

Her frightening dreams were filled with action and suspense. Out of a gray haze, a coiled snake reared its ugly head and lunged toward her, baring its fangs. In her dream, Esy pulled away, thwarting the venomous attack. She sprinted in an attempt to outrun the creature. Esy quaked with fright when another confrontation ensued. Terrified, wet with sweat and gasping for breath, she woke, ending her nightmare.

After she realized where she was, Esy shook her head, grateful that it was just a bad dream. She checked the sun and it was high in the sky, so she hoped David was back in his office. After washing and putting on her laundered dress, Esy went to the kitchen to find something to fill her empty stomach. Plantains and hard-boiled eggs would give her the energy she needed to keep going. She knocked on David's door.

"Hello, Esy," he said smiling. "What brings you here?"

She plopped herself in a chair and told him the whole story. David listened intently without interrupting her. Esy shared her disappointment with Daddy Dayana and his insatiable need for money to feed his gambling life. They discussed the charlatans, Hackett Salomon and Viktor von Peeters. David nodded his head in understanding.

"You are a smart girl." David said. "You figured out what they wanted and it was not to get you an education. What are you going to do, now?"

"I'm not sure." Esy responded. "When Asha comes

home from the mine, we're going to try to find Mama's journal in my old bedroom. I know what I *don't want to do.*"

"That's a start. If you need my help, I'll do what I can."

"You have been helpful already. Thank you." Esy gave him a hug and left his office. Finding that same chair she curled up in the night before, she sat and waited for Asha. Esy knew that she did *not* want to work in the mine anymore just to feed Daddy Dayana's habit. The last couple of days had tested her, so she was confident she could survive on her own. David said she was smart and Esy considered herself shrewd, at least some of the time. Getting an education was at the top of her list. After that, she wanted to help her brother Moyo find his way in the world.

Asha came back from her work. She smiled at her dear friend and was ready to make the long trek back to the mission station at the Ruashi mine. As they walked down the rill-damaged road, Esy grabbed her friend's hand and together, the two young girls started their long journey. It was a sixteen-kilometer trip traveling over a stony road filled with potholes. They suffered the blazing late afternoon sun with no water, one of their biggest hardships. Their mouths were dry and their lips parched. Esy prayed that her mother's journal would still be there under her bed. This would make their difficult trek worthwhile.

It was nightfall when they arrived at the mission. The overseers of this station, Jackson and Angela, were not as compassionate as David and Mary Ann. When they first saw Esy, they crossly demanded to know where she had been.

"I spent some time at the mission by the Etoile mine," she said torn between telling a fib to protect herself or divulging the truth.

The owners of the Ruashi mine were generous contributors to the Baptist mission stations. They supplied money for their endeavors, which was taking care of the children—their workers. That way, they could maintain control over the comings and goings of the children who worked in the mine. It was the kind of arrangement where I'll help you out if you help us out. The children were business commodities since they found the valuable cobalt in the piles of smelting remnants. The owners of the mine needed someone to keep track of their whereabouts. A few of the missionaries acted as agents of the mines.

"Your daddy and Hackett Salomon have been looking for you," Jackson remarked, looking down his nose at her. "We couldn't give them any information, because you didn't communicate with us before you left."

"I left some things in my room I want to get," Esy said.

"Well, I'm afraid Dayana and Hackett took everything out of there."

Esy's heart sank, she could feel her knees weaken as though she would faint. Her friend steadied her.

"Esy would like to make sure they didn't miss anything," Asha said.

"Okay," Jackson said. "Make it quick."

Asha guided Esy to her room, holding onto her to keep her upright. The room was totally bare. Esy was sure they had taken the journal. She sprang into action by looking under the mattress supported by woven banana leaves. She found it where she had left it. So excited, she hugged Asha and they did a little jig together as Esy clutched her journal to her chest. They skipped out of the mission station hoping never to return to that dismal unwelcoming place. It was night and they had a long trip ahead of them.

The full moon rose higher in the night sky as they walked together in silence, wary of their surroundings. Finally, as they drew closer to the city, Esy stopped, and looked at her friend.

"Asha, I want to check on a house in Elisabethville that my mother mentioned in her journal," Esy entreated.

"Why?"

"My mother was raised in that house and I wonder if it's still there."

"Is it far from here?" Asha asked. "I'm getting tired."

"No, it's just around the corner."

The two friends found the house at 100 Ave des Sapiniers, in a nice part of town. It was a lovely little yellow house with a white door and shutters with Hibiscus bushes growing along the porch. Lights were on and there was activity inside. It had a welcoming feel. Esy's eyes stared longingly at the little house across the street, yearning to meet the people inside. *I don't think it's Amelia and Bertrand – they would be too old—but maybe the people who live there now would know them.* She hoped to work up enough courage to knock on the door. But that would have to wait until morning. Tonight, the two friends needed to find a place to sleep. Maybe there was a park nearby with a bench. They would walk until they found one.

Morning painted the sky with red hues and nature was all around her when Esy opened her eyes. Even though the bench in the park was small and hard, they'd slept well enough to feel ready to start on the long journey home. Esy was hungry, but with no money in her pocket, they would have to find something to eat they could pick from a tree. Mangoes were ripe that time of year, and would taste so good. Esy scoured the park for fruit and found a small, scrappy-looking mango tree with decent fruit. Once they had eaten their fill, they were ready to start the day. Asha needed to get back to the mine, but Esy wanted to meet the people who lived in the yellow house, so they parted company. As she watched her friend walk down the dusty road toward the mine, she hoped that life in the mine would not be her fate. Summoning all of her courage, she walked toward the little yellow house.

Lights were on, so they were waking up. Esy's insides were shaking. She wanted to knock on the front door, but was frozen with fear. She took a step forward, and then hesitated. *What if the person inside is mean to me or calls the police? What would I do? Could I run away? Probably they could outrun me. Would they take away the little freedom I do have? I'm just a poor orphan girl. Why do I think I deserve an education? Do I matter to anyone? I'm not ready to do this.*

Defeated, Esy doggedly headed back to the mission station. She hoped David and Mary Ann would be there. It had been a frustrating day and she was on the verge of tears.

"Hi, Mary Ann," Esy said forcing her tears back. But, they came out anyway as she sobbed in Mary Ann's arms.

"What's wrong? Did you not find your journal?" Mary Ann said while holding Esy on her lap enfolded in her arms.

"Yes, it was under my bed, but I'm so afraid. There is something that is so important to me, and I don't have the courage to do it."

"What's that?"

"Mama lived with a Belgian couple, Amelia and Bertrand, as a housemaid when she was my age. Amelia helped her with reading, math and science. I went by their house in Elisabethville today on the way back. It looked like someone was inside, but I was too afraid to go to the door and knock. I don't have the courage."

"Esy, you are courageous!" Mary Ann said. "You're so young and you've done so many grown-up tasks. Why do you want to meet Amelia and Bertrand?"

"I want to know more about Mama. They probably don't live there anymore, but the people who do live there might know them. Secretly, I hope they'll be able to help me go to school to become educated like Mama."

"Education matters a lot to you, doesn't it? Let me talk to David—he might have some ideas. He'll be home later this evening. Let's plan on meeting at breakfast tomorrow."

Esy appreciated Mary Ann's wisdom and her kindness. Exhausted from the hard crying and the emotional upset, Esy was ready for a sound, healing sleep.

ೞೞೞ

"Good morning, Esy," David said motioning that she should sit in the chair next to him. "Mary Ann mentioned you wanted to meet your mother's Belgian parents to learn more about her."

"Yes, I want to discover who she was. And I hope they can help me become educated the way they helped my mother."

"I don't want you to be disappointed. More than likely they don't live there anymore."

"You're probably right, but that house pulls me toward it like a magnet."

"Would you like me or Mary Ann to go with you?"

"Thank you, I would."

"Also, I want you to know that I have talked with a friend of mine who works for the schools in Elisabethville and he said that there is a program sponsored by the Colonial government that gives scholarships to African children who want to go school. He thought you might qualify."

Esy's eyes opened wide and a smile brightened her face.

"I have some time tomorrow afternoon and the mission van will be available, let's take a ride."

"I hope. I hope I can get educated," Esy said as she jumped up and down so excited about the possibility. Her childlike joy made David chuckle.

ᘓᘓᘓ

The next day couldn't come soon enough for Esy, and with David supporting her she was full of courage. Right after breakfast, David and Esy climbed into the dusty old van and headed to 100 Ave des Sapiniers. Bouncing along the bumpy, dusty roads, David and Esy started singing the familiar tunes they sang around the table at dinnertime. It was a happy ride. David drove up next to the house, but they were disappointed to find nobody home. They knocked three times, but no response. Dejected, they headed back to the van.

"While we're here in Elisabethville let's see if my friend, who knows about the scholarships, is in his office." The two of them went to the University of Elisabethville just a few blocks away. As they approached the main building, Esy was intimidated by the size of the five-story building. Large groups of students were mingling and walking on the tamped red earth surrounding the building. Esy was certain that she could not brave this on her own and was thankful that David was willing to help her. They took the stairs to the third floor and walked to an information desk and asked to speak to Paul Gaster. The receptionist made a phone call and had them take a seat in the waiting room. Paul arrived and walked right up to David.

"This is Esy, the eager student that I talked to you about," David said.

"Hi, my name is Paul," the man said as he shook her hand. "Come into my office." Both David and Esy followed him into a small office filled from top to bottom with books. "So why do you want to get an education?"

"Mama said that education helped her understand the world and she wanted me to learn what she learned."

"Was your mother African?"

"Yes, she was a servant girl for Amelia, who was a schoolteacher in Belgium. She taught Mama to read, do math and study science."

"Is your father African?"

"Yes, Daddy Dayana works in the Ruashi mine."

"The reason I'm asking this is because being completely African is a requirement for the scholarship," Paul said. "The next step is for you to be tested. Frieda Van Tyl does that part of the process. I'll give her a call to set up an appointment for the testing. What time works for you?"

"Afternoons work best for me," David said.

"Okay, I'll let you know when I arrange the time." He shook hands with David and Esy and said good-bye.

Other than some trepidation about the test, Esy was jubilant during the ride home and David was upbeat too. They felt certain this would work out. Esy could live at the mission station and either get a ride with David or walk the distance to school. It was about a two-kilometer walk, but she was sure she could do it.

CRCRCR

The day came for the scheduled test. Esy had the jitters wondering how hard the test would be and she didn't know what to study because it was all new to her. David drove Esy to the University of Elisabethville early in the day because he had to meet another missionary at the airport who just arrived from the United States. This meant Esy had several hours to fill before she had to take the test. The house at 100 Ave des Sapiniers called to her and her curiosity got the better of her. Emboldened by the possibility of getting a scholarship, she found the courage to walk right up to the front door and knock. The door opened.

Her heart beat hard against the walls of her chest, but she stayed focused on her mission. What she saw in front of her was a haggard middle-aged woman with a sad face. Her wrinkles around her mouth were in a permanent frown making her look unhappy. Her hair was unkempt and the noisome smell of cigarette smoke emanated from every nook and cranny of her house.

"Hello," Esy said, her voice faltering. "My name is Esynama. My mother lived in this house with Bertrand and Amelia a while back and I'm wondering if you know them."

"We bought the house from them," she said after an uncomfortable pause. "They moved back to Belgium when Bertrand retired from the mine."

"I would like to write to Amelia. I want to know more about my mama. Do you have her address?"

"I don't, but my husband might. He's on a business trip and won't be back for a couple of days. I'll ask him when he gets home."

"Thank you. I'll stop by later in the week. I have to take

a test for a scholarship, so I have to get to the University. Where is it from here?"

"It's two blocks south, turn right for another three blocks. It would be on your left," she said, pointing down the street.

"Thank you so much for the information," Esy said. "Good bye." She probably could have found it on her own, but the neighborhood was unfamiliar. She arrived at the place where she had to turn right and saw the big five-story building. The building loomed large. She opened the glass door and went inside planning to ask anybody walking the halls where she could find Frieda Van Tyl. Without David by her side, the sight of all the older students intimidated her. She was the youngest one there. Feeling an urge to walk back outside, she mustered all her courage to press on. Sensing her consternation, a young man asked if she needed help.

"I need to find Frieda Van Tyl's office." Esy said. "Where can I find her?"

He gave her a friendly smile and said, "Follow me."

Esy followed him right into an elevator. She'd never ridden in an elevator before. The momentum of the large box and the sucking sound of the movement upward terrified her. She prayed to God for more courage, but was relieved when the door opened to another floor. The young man pointed in the direction of Frieda Van Tyl's office and Esy smiled and thanked him with a nod.

"I'd like to speak with Frieda Van Tyl," she said to a person behind a desk. The receptionist motioned for her to sit down. Esy waited a very long time. It must have been late in the day because the sun was coming through the west windows.

"Hello," said a husky voice. "I'm Frieda Van Tyl. How can I help you?"

"I'm Esynama. David's friend scheduled an appointment for me."

"Ah, yes. Paul called me to set up that appointment. Come into my office and we can start the testing."

Maybe this is my lucky break. I must look smart.

"So, how old are you?"

"I'll be twelve next month."

"Have you ever been to school?"

"No. My mother taught me everything I know," Esy said brightly. "Mama was taught by Amelia Franken who was from Belgium. Amelia taught her English, French, literature, history and math, and then, Mama taught me all she knew. I translated a letter in English for Hackett Salomon, the boss of the Ruashi mine.

"I know Hackett. Let's see, I must check with a school in Elisabethville about what testing they want. Please come back in two days about the same time of day and in the meantime I'll give the school a call."

Esy smiled, thanked her, and left for the mission station to tell Asha, Mary Ann, and David what happened. She felt strangely free and hopeful. It took her no time at all to get to the mission station. As she was approaching, she saw David waving and gesturing for her to go away. Confused by his strange behavior, Esy stopped dead in her tracks. She had nowhere to go. Her only recourse was to climb high in a Baobab tree on the property and watch. Fixing her eyes on the front door, she saw quick movements flashing by the windows and heard some shouting. She waited.

Hackett Salomon burst through the door, slamming it

behind him. Esy watched until he got in his vehicle and erratically drove down the road like a man possessed, and when she was sure he was gone, she climbed down.

Esy walked without stopping to Asha's room. She opened the door and panicked when she saw Daddy Dayana sitting on her friend's bed waiting for her. Her heart pounded madly in her chest—she felt faint, and everything went blank.

When she awoke, Daddy Dayana was holding her in his arms, smiling at her. *I don't think he's mad at me. I hope he doesn't want me to go back to the mine.*

"Hi, Daddy," she said. The way he held her now reminded her of how he used to carry her when she was a child.

"What has mtoto wa kike been doing?" Daddy asked.

Esy carefully explained her desire to be educated, and how Mama Mary encouraged her to find a way to go to school. Most of all, Esy emphasized that she did *not* want to go back to the mine. She shared the encounter she had with Frieda Van Tyl and that she planned to meet with her again in two days. Daddy listened, nodding his head.

"You are a good mineworker," Daddy Dayana said. "Hackett and I would like to see you back at the Ruashi mine."

"I want to see how this works with Frieda Van Tyl," Esy responded. "If nothing happens, then, maybe I'll go back to the mine. If I get that scholarship, I won't be working in the mine. You'll have to find some other way to get money because I won't be able to give you money."

"I might have Moyo work in the mines instead of you."

"No, No! I don't want my brother to work in the mines," Esy exclaimed, starting to cry.

"Esy, *you* don't have any *say* in the matter," Daddy

chuckled. "It's the *only* way children can make money here in the Katanga province. I have to get back to the mine—Hackett is waiting for me. Let me know how it turns out with the testing."

"Good-bye, Daddy." Esy tried to give her father a hug, but he just walked away from her.

Esy flopped on her bed and curled up like a baby. She was exhausted by the swirling emotions of the day. She had taken the first step toward getting an education—which made her happy. She had the courage to knock on the door of Mama's old house and was eagerly anticipating the next appointment with Frieda Van Tyl.

Esy didn't wake up when Asha returned from her day's work at the mine. When she eventually did wake up the next morning, she was so hungry she ate a full breakfast of cassava bread, boiled eggs, a plantain, and mango slices. Mary Ann came out of the kitchen and asked her how she was doing. Esy told her about the possibility of going to school, but explained that she had to take some tests first. Mary Ann gave her a blessing, which Esy received in full measure.

"Esy, you have a wonderful opportunity and your direction is a good one," Mary Ann said. "It will take a lot of hard work, perseverance, and doing your best. Your strength will be tested, so stay strong."

ભ ભ ભ

The time to meet with Frieda Van Tyl finally came. Esy waited outside her office for a long time before she was called in.

"I have good news," Frieda said. "I called a school, which is just a block from the university and they have an opening for you. We should know more after the test which grade is best for you. Are you ready to take the test?"

"Yes," Esy said.

Mary Ann's words keep coming back—"Do your best and stay strong."

Esy gave the test everything she had. She pushed through her anxiety and fear, and just stayed as focused as she could. Mary Ann had given her several pencils and an eraser. She also reminded her to ask questions about how to do the test *before* she started writing, and stressed the importance of listening to the directions.

Esy waited for the results, which seemed like forever. Finally, Frieda tallied the results; some scores were very good and others were not. Esy received the highest scores in the French and English languages, her science scores were quite high, but she had very low scores in mathematics.

"You did well, especially for not going to school," Frieda said. "You will be at the high school level in languages and science, but you'll be at the fourth grade level in math. The school that has an opening is Ecole Internationale. The school is just a few blocks from here and they have all the grades in one building. If you study hard, you can advance to the next grade."

Esy's eyes widened, and she wiggled in her chair. She could hardly contain herself. She was grateful that the low scores didn't hold her back and Esy was so ready to get started.

"There is one problem – you need money for books," Frieda said. "The scholarship will pay for the tuition, but the supplies and the books you or your parents need to buy. Do you have anyone that will help you pay for them?"

"I have *no* money," Esy said, her spirits plunging. "My

daddy gambles away the money I give him from mining and selling cobalt."

Frieda's shoulders tensed and her face was expressionless. She rose without commenting, walked to another room and shut the door behind her. Esy heard her dial a phone followed by a muffled conversation. She strained to hear, but couldn't understand the words. When Frieda returned, she looked directly at Esy.

"My friend Stella is willing to have you live with her and Russell. They are looking for a servant. You'll work for your room and board," Frieda said smiling. "*And*, they are willing to pay for your books and supplies."

"Who are Stella and Russell?"

"They live about six blocks from here. Russell is an engineer at the Etoile mine." They are from Belgium and live on Sapiniers Ave. I'll draw you a map.

"Oh, thank you," Esy said. She was dumbfounded. *Could it be that I will be working and living in a house on the same street that Mama did many years ago? God heard my cries, and answered me. Mama Mary and her journal have been so helpful. It's a miracle.*

"Your classes will start Monday of next week. Stella said you could move in this weekend. She lives at 100 Sapiniers Ave. and I suggest you talk with her soon. The best of everything to you," Frieda said as she dropped her no nonsense business demeanor by giving her a hug.

I'm certain that the house is where Mama lived. I must talk to Stella today.

જીજીજી

The directions to the little yellow house were etched in her memory. She knocked on the door and waited. To her surprise, Stella had freshened up and was an impressive looking woman. Snow white hair with dark brown eyebrows and ruby red lips gave her a sophisticated look. Esy looked down at her own dress, thinking it wasn't very fine.

"Hello, Esynama,"Stella said. "Welcome to my home. You've been here before, so it is meant to be."

"Thank you for your kindness," Esy said, looking at the floor.

"Come, child. I'll show you your room."

Esy followed Stella downstairs to a basement room that had a small window where she could look outside. It had a bed, with a fluffy white cover, pink pillows, and furry stuffed animals near the headboard. A kitten peaked out from under the bed skirt.

"Oh, that's Patch," Stella said. "Do you like cats?"

"I do, but I've never had one where I sleep."

"Let me show you the bathroom, which is next to your bedroom."

"Bathroom? What's that?" Esy only knew a bafuni as a hole in a cement floor where you had to squat. Wearing a dress made it easier to go. This bathroom had a white hole that was raised with water in it, so you could sit in comfort. The sink was another curiosity. Instead of a water pump, which splashed on your legs and feet while you washed your hands, this bathroom had a place to wash, which was at your height, so your legs stayed dry. Amazing. Esy liked all of the new comforts, but was even more excited about getting to school to "get educated," as Mama advised in her journal.

"You will have jobs to do around the house and yard," Stella said. "Do you know how to cook?"

"Yes, Mama Mary taught me how to cook all the African food," Esy said. "And, she showed me how to set a table and serve food. Amelia taught her, so Mama showed me."

"Good. I'll have you cook the evening meals for us," Stella declared. "How about cleaning and gardening?"

"I can do that."

"During the day, your job will be go to classes and study hard. You received some scholarship money, but Russell and I will be paying for books and supplies, so we are investing in you."

Esy smiled and nodded. "When do you want me to move in?"

"As soon as you can."

"I left some clothes at the mission near the Etoile mine I need to get, but I'll be back tomorrow.

ೞೞೞ

Excited to start her new life, Esy's spirit felt lighter than air. As she headed back to the mission station, confusing thoughts began to temper her joy. *Everything seemed too perfect. I have never had an experience like this in my life. When my life was going well, bad things happened to me. My home life was happy but then, Mama got sick, and when Daddy pulled away from the family, I was yanked to the mine. The mine was such a wretched place. I coughed from the cobalt dust and my fingers bled from picking the cobalt out of the copper and nickel. Worst of all, Mama died and I lost someone who cared deeply for me. Then, Hackett with his giant belly and big nose poked at me wanting to use me for his evil ways. Stella, David, Paul have given me so much hope for schooling so I can have a better life but I don't trust what's happening to me. Is it a miracle or is it just another way I'll be used for someone's selfish designs?*

ର୍ଷ୍ଠର୍ଷ୍ଠର୍ଷ୍ଠ

Supper at the mission was pleasant. Esy considered Asha, Mary Ann, and David to be like family. She loved them and they had been her support through all the ups and downs. The rumpus of a soccer game was the usual activity before and after supper. Infectious laughter and good-humored teasing filled the place with joy. She had grown comfortable with the other children at the mission station. The idea of living with Stella and Russell was an unknown and a bit scary. *I wonder if Stella will be like a mother to me and her husband like a father? I am grateful they are being kind to me but I just don't know what to expect.*

" I met your brother today," Asha said.

"Where?" Esy asked.

"He was in the middle of a group of boys on the way to the mine."

"Did he look okay?"

"Yes, he was jokin' around and teasing one of the boys."

"How did you know it was him?"

"His friend shouted, 'Moyo, Moyo,' and I remember you calling him by that name."

"If you see him again, let him know that I want to talk to him—give him my new address."

Esy scribbled Stella and Russell's address on a piece of paper and handed it to her. She hoped her dear brother would come to visit her soon because she missed him so much. She was angry with her father for having Moyo replace her in the mine. In her alone times, she raged at Daddy Dayana because he used his children to make money for his disreputable life.

Esy spent time with Asha describing her new home and the school she planned to attend. When Asha heard about her plans to go to school, she looked sad and a shade jealous. Esy hoped that someday her friend would be able to go to school too. Esy knew that she had to take care of herself right now, so providing a better life for Moyo and Asha would have to come later after she finished school.

After saying her good-byes to all her friends, she turned around to leave— ready to embark on a new life. She knew in just a few days she would face dramatic changes. She would sleep in a bed with a fluffy white bedspread, use a toilet, wash her face and hands in a sink, and snuggle with Patch. It was a dream come true! Her school experience was still a mystery to her. *I wonder what the teachers will be like and the other students? Will the subjects be hard or easy? What will the textbooks be like? What will I wear? What kind of food will I eat? I have so much to learn, but I'm excited to find out. As Mary Ann said,* "stay strong"—*I will, Mary Ann. I will.*

She quickened her steps as she approached the little yellow house, knocked on the door, and waited.

"Who's there?" Stella shouted.

"It is Esynama," she said, confused by Stella's now gruff voice, a voice that had been so pleasant the day before.

"You don't need to knock, you live here now, so just walk-in."

Her change in mood made Esy uneasy. She opened the door, and Stella was smoking and drinking in the kitchen. Those behaviors were forbidden in the Kimbanquist religion, so, right from the start, Esy felt like she didn't fit in. *Oh, no what is going to happen to me?* She hadn't learned the rules of being a servant at Stella's house, but that would come soon enough. She nodded to Stella and went downstairs to her room, looking for Patch.

Pulling up the side of her fluffy bedspread, she spotted two glowing eyes. Esy giggled with delight. She reached out to grab the cat, but Patch slipped away into the darkness under the bed. She considered the possibility that Patch might be afraid too, so instead of getting upset, she started organizing her room.

There were enough windows in the basement to make the lower level cheery enough. Taking the folded clothes out of her bag, she looked for a place to store them. By the wall in her bedroom, there was a large wooden rectangular box. She pulled on the handles and found empty space inside, so she placed her clothes there. How convenient not to have to put her clothes on a chair to keep them off the floor. It was a novelty to shut the drawers knowing her clothes would be there when she needed them.

On the other wall was an unmarked door, which she opened. Triangular wires dangled from a pole inside the closet. *They look so strange—I wonder what they're used for. I'll ask Stella about them.*

"Hi, Stella," Esy said after climbing the stairs. "When would you like me to make supper?"

"It's just the two of us," Stella responded. "My husband won't be back until after the weekend, on Wednesday."

"I can make some salt fish and cassava bread. Would you like that?"

"Yes, that sounds good."

Esy made dinner, grateful that her Mama had taught her how to make a good meal. With the food cooked, table set, and the serving bowls filled, Esy told Stella that dinner was ready. Drowsy from the alcohol, Stella struggled to get out of her chair to the dining room table. Esy tried hard to be patient, but she was concerned about Stella's lifestyle. Esy knew she should just be quiet, but it irked her to see Stella undermining her own health, and so she spoke up.

"I was raised a Kimbanquist," Esy said. "We don't believe in smoking *or* drinking alcohol."

"What are you saying?" Stella snapped. "Are you saying I'm living wrong?"

"Yes," Esy retorted. "There's a reason why it's forbidden."

"You don't understand what I have to endure with my husband!" Stella screeched. "Go to your room—you sassy little upstart."

Esy was stunned by her outburst. Frightened that everything would fall apart, she hastily ran downstairs to her basement bedroom. *I was just trying to be helpful. Didn't Stella understand that? Sometimes I'm so dumb and I don't think about what I'm saying.* Esy curled up on her bed and spent several tear-filled hours alone sobbing in her room not knowing what had gone so wrong.

This was a hard lesson, but, she learned the first rule of being a servant—never, *never* criticize your mistress. *I wonder why learning has to be so painful. Am I going to be able to survive this?* Esy decided not to talk to Stella that night, but would apologize to her the next morning after breakfast.

Stella was in much better shape the next morning and, when Esy came upstairs, she asked her if she wanted to go to Mass with her at ten. Esy nodded, freshened up and put on her best dress. *I wonder if Stella forgot about what I said last night. I'm not going to bring it up unless she does.* Going off to church together was a new, shared adventure for Esy and Stella, and thankfully, Stella didn't mention Esy's impertinence the night before.

As they walked up the stairs to the St. Peter and Paul Cathedral, Esy could feel the reverence of the parishioners. A host of believers joined the throngs inside of what was the most intriguing church building she had ever seen. The stone on the outside of the cathedral matched the red dirt found in the countryside. Once they went inside, the archways and the light streaming through the series of rectangular windows encircled them, creating a jubilant environment. Esy glanced at Stella's face while she was worshiping, and was happy to see how peaceful she looked.

There were differences between what the Catholic Church taught and the teachings of the Kimbanquists. The Kimbanquist's religion was vehemently against smoking, drinking, dancing, and violence of any kind. It discouraged wearing shoes and abhorred polygamy. Ironically, the wrongs of gambling and exploiting young children for money received little mention. The Catholic Mass was reverent and worshipful. Knowing that Christ was the center of both the Catholic and Kimbanquist's services comforted her. She told Stella she wanted to attend Mass again. Many beliefs of the Kimbanquist religion made little sense. *Other religions have good parts to them. I want to know more.*

ରେରେରେ

The principal of the school Esy attended, André Labon, introduced himself and welcomed her. The school building was a lovely brick place with two floors of classrooms surrounded by grounds that were almost park-like. The principal was a slight, energetic fellow seemingly well liked by the students. There were plenty of friendly greetings exchanged between the students and the principal before the school day started. He took a few minutes to go over her class schedule but Esy, after looking around at the other students, noticed that all of the students dressed alike. Esy wanted to fit in and she knew that she had to dress like everyone else.

"I'm not wearing what everyone else is wearing. Where do I get those clothes?"

The principal nodded and had his secretary find the right sized uniform for her in the closet in her office. Feeling the confidence of fitting in, Esy held her head high as she went to her first class. She felt some comfort knowing her outfit matched, but little did they know that her insides were shaking.

There were only sixteen students in her first class, which was English. She looked around to see if there might be a familiar face—they were all strangers only similar in age. Most had white faces, but there were a few black ones. *I wonder how many of them have lost their mother? Has anybody here had to work in the mine to make money for their father? Does anyone have a cat like Patch for a pet?* Her teacher taught the entire class in English. Mama Mary had taught her well; she understood almost every word her teacher said.

The assignment was to write a story. *I want to write the best story in the class. I will work hard. Maybe Stella can help me. I'll check on Stella's mood before I ask her.* Esy was certain she would be a good student, a successful contender, since she was good at languages. Even Frieda Van Tyl said so. She was a little worried about being able to do all the homework. Esy knew she would have to find a way.

Esy's first day of school brought her such joy because she knew her Mama would be proud. She skipped all the way back to the little yellow house, taking in the neighborhood sights and sounds. There were a few students walking from school down the street where she lived. The row of houses were freshly painted with lovely flowers in the front yard. She was proud to be part of this new neighborhood. A sweet, warm smell greeted her as she opened the door. The delicious smell led her to the kitchen. Perhaps, Stella was making something tasty. Indeed, she was baking and seemed to be as excited as Esy was about the start of school.

"I remember my mother making cookies for me when I was in school." Stella reminisced. "I enjoyed coming through the front door, tantalized by luscious smells. I hope you like my Speculoos cookies."

"They smell so good." Esy said as she sat at the table with a glass of milk and two warm cookies. She gingerly took the first bite of cookie and closed her eyes. "Yum! It's so *sweet*! What is it made of?"

"I'll bet the taste you like is the brown sugar," Stella answered.

Esy devoured the cookies and drank some of the milk. "Could I have another cookie?"

"Of course," Stella said with a happy chuckle. "I'm glad you like them."

Esy and Stella were off to a good start. It was "happy Stella" that greeted her. Would this last? Only the future would tell.

CHAPTER 5

Russell Cox

ಐಐಐಐ

A red, drop-top Austin Healy Sprite raced up the driveway on Wednesday of that week. A cute little car, its fans
dubbed it the "Frogeye" because the headlights protruded
like a frog's eyes. Russell Cox was home from his business
trip. He jumped out of the car without opening the door.
Stella's husband was a tall man with a shock of red hair
and a casual gait. He exuded fun and amiability. Russell cruised into the house, kissed Stella, found the most
comfortable chair in the house, and lit up a cigarette.

"How's my girl?" he asked.

"Happy to see you, love," Stella said, with a coquett-
ish smile. She sat in the chair next to him, took a cigarette out of his shirt pocket, and lit up. They chatted and
played like two kids.

Esy opened the front door to find the two of them kiss-
ing and sharing sweet nothings. Russell looked up and
watched her come through the door.

"Well well," he said. "What have we here?"

"It's a long story. I'll fill you in later," Stella said.

"Come here and shake my hand, young lady."

Esy walked toward him with downcast eyes and slow steps. She was most uncomfortable—not sure if he approved of her. She felt like she was an interruption. Honey words were not something she saw or heard from her Mama and Daddy. They worked and went to church, but she didn't see much affection. Stella and Russell were very different.

"Welcome to our home," he said, sounding sincere.

"Thank you," Esy said, as she scurried downstairs to her bedroom to find Patch. Her self-conscious feelings made her blush. Russell and Stella had their own secret language and she wasn't able to understand it.

Where do I fit in? How can I manage this different life? She knew for certain that doing well in school by finishing her homework was what Stella wanted. Studying and getting good grades was the one concrete something she could hang onto in her uncertain world. It was her ticket to a brighter future and she instinctively knew that. Being a good student made her fit in, and she decided that would be her focus.

As she set her books down, she noticed that her hands were healed from the gashes she got from cobalt mining. There were a few scars left from the deep cuts, but her hands were getting softer and more genteel. It was a relief not having to go to the mine to work and she noticed she hadn't been coughing as much during the night since she started school. She smiled and nodded to herself knowing she was headed in the right direction.

"Esy," Stella yelled down the stairs. "Russ and I will be going out for supper, so you're off duty tonight."

"Okay, see you later."

Esy prepared a light supper of leftovers and went to her room to continue her studies. She had hoped to ask Stella to critique her story, but now that Russell was home, she would have to find someone else. Her English teacher might be able to give her suggestions about somebody who could help her when she needed it. Her work had to be as perfect as possible.

As she was nodding off to sleep late in the evening with Patch on the pillow next to hers, Esy heard footsteps clomping on the floor above her, along with an occasional burst of laughter. Russell and Stella were home after a long evening. An eerie quiet followed their noisy return and then, sudden, violent animal sounds pierced the dark. She recalled hearing those sounds during the night when she was a child. She pulled Patch closer, and tried to sleep.

The next morning, after grabbing a plantain for breakfast, Esy tiptoed out of the house so she wouldn't wake them. She could hear snoring sounds coming from their bedroom. Going to school was still a wonder-filled adventure and something she would handle with the greatest care. Only two more days and she would have finished her first week of school.

ଓଓଓ

So far, her experience at school was better than expected and Esy beamed with pride when she got her first paper back. She had all the answers right and she received one-hundred percent. In her history class she learned that the major cities of Elisabethville, Judotville, and Leopoldville had held the first independent elections in 1957, but only adult males could vote. Women had no voting rights during those elections. She learned that, for the first time during her lifetime, emancipation and decolonization from Belgium were being discussed. It was possible she would see the Belgian Congo become an independent country. Esy wished her Mama could have lived long enough to see the African identity and freedom come to her beloved country. The history of the Belgian Congo fascinated her.

The bell rang, signaling that school was out—Esy's first week was over. *I wonder what the weekend will be like with Russell and Stella. I want to make a good meal for them tonight; maybe Stella will have some ideas.* When Esy got home, the house was empty. The little red car was not in the driveway. Were Stella and Russell out together, or did Russell go on another business trip? Stella did not let her know they would be gone for dinner, so she decided to prepare dinner for them anyway. Esy checked the cupboards to find food for supper. She liked being creative with her cooking.

"I know what I'll serve," Esy said talking to herself. "I'd like to make some chikwanga for Russell—I don't think he's ever had it."

She found canned chicken, cassava flour and palm nuts in the cupboard. I know, *I could make Poulet á la Moambé with chikwanga.* Esy proceeded to make a delicious meal for Stella and Russell. She set the table and readied the serving dishes for food.

The little red car roared up the driveway as the brakes

screeched a halt. They had arrived. Boisterous laughter preceded them as they entered the house.

"What smells so good?" Russell asked.

"I'm making chicken with palm oil sauce and chikwanga."

"What in the heck is chikwanga?"

"It's cassava cooked in banana leaves," Esy said.

"Are we ready to eat?" Stella asked.

"The chikwanga will be done in a few minutes." Esy filled the serving dishes with steaming food fit for a king and queen. Stella and Russell asked Esy about her first week of school while they enjoyed the meal. Esy described her teachers, summarized the classes, and shared parts of the story she wrote for her English class. *I like this—it feels like we're a family*

"Would you like a ride in my car?" Russell asked.

Esy giggled. "I've never ridden in a car before, but I *have* to clean up the kitchen."

"I'll clean up for you tonight," Stella said. "You two have a good time."

"Oh, thank you," Esy said with enthusiasm. "Yes, I would like a ride."

Her feet tapped the floor and she did a little jig all the way to the car. Russell chuckled over her antics as he climbed over the door and revved up the engine. Esy copied him by climbing over the door too. Russell drove with reckless disregard for safety, which made Esy excited and panic-stricken at the same time. She hung onto the door handle with all her might to keep steady. Russell clipped the corners fast and close and pushed the gas pedal to the floor. Esy swayed from side to side and lunged back and forth. Russell hit a pothole, and the car popped up in the air. Esy levitated way above her comfort level. Her nervous laughter was infectious because Russell joined in by laughing, too. Undaunted by her worry, he continued up the side of the mountain as reckless as ever.

He pulled over to the side of the road and parked. He walked around the car and lifted Esy up and over the passenger door, winking and smiling at her. After holding her up in the air a moment, he set her down and turned around. Together they looked at a beautiful view of the town of Elisabethville. He pointed to the boulevard that was in front of the little yellow house, and to a small, single-engine plane taking off from the airport. The scene high above the city was lovelier than a close-up view.

The sun was setting, and it was time to go home. Not knowing how to open the car door, Esy waited for Russell to open it. Instead, he picked her up, tickled her, and set her in the passenger seat without opening the door. She giggled.

"Are you ticklish?"

"Yes, very, but I'm not telling you where," Esy said. His familiar manner was confusing to her.

The return trip was more subdued. For Esy, the newness had worn off. When they got home, she thanked Russell for the ride and went downstairs to her room to play with Patch. *Russell is fun loving—a little bit crazy. I've never had an experience like that before. I didn't know if I was going to live or die. I wonder if he plays soccer that way, too.*

Esy readied for bed and took her mother's journal out from under the mattress. She hadn't read it since she moved into Stella and Russell's house, but the day's events made her wish for her mother's guidance.

My Dear Esy,

I have lived with a conflict my whole life and I suspect you will suffer the same fate. So far, in this life, I have learned how to be a slave, subservient to my masters, my mistress, and my husband. In the book of Ephesians in the Bible, Paul talks about slaves:

"Slaves, obey your earthly masters with deep respect and fear. Serve them sincerely, as you would serve Christ." Ephesians 6:5

I have done what it says in the Bible. I served Amelia, Bertrand, and Dayana, and of course I took care of my children, who I love so much.

In a perfect world, man and woman, slave and master should be equal, serving each other without one of them being dominant. Maybe that will only happen in heaven, I don't know.

But, I do know that women need to be empowered by using the best tool available—education. In an ideal world, women don't have to be subservient to anyone. I hope and pray that the role of women will change for you. It will be a slow process, but if you don't give-up the fight, progress is sure.

Love always,

Mama Mary

Esy scratched her head. This time she didn't fully grasp what she read—it was a message that was hard to understand. She understood the education part but that was it. Her eyelids were heavy and she was ready for sleep. She would think about it another time and maybe it would become clearer to her as she got older.

CRCRCR

That car ride changed Esy and Russell's relationship. They were like playmates, fun loving and easy. Stella liked having Esy around—it lightened things up. Esy seemed to be the child they always wanted, but couldn't have. Not being able to have children was major problem and Stella thought of her barren condition as calamitous. Crippling grief would creep into her soul and she would become depressed, which would take a long time to shake.

Esy's sunny disposition helped Stella climb out of that dark place. Stella found a new purpose by making cookies to share with Esy after school. The good memories of her childhood came to mind. Life felt more complete than it ever had before. It was good to have a young one in the house.

Esy continued to balance her work at home and her homework for school nicely. She did well in school, but Stella had only one worry about Esy. She didn't seem to have any friends who would come to visit her after school and her only true friend was Patch. The cat and Esy bonded like glue. They played tag through the house, they slept together, and often, Stella would hear her talk to Patch. Stella chose to be patient but encouraged her to bring a friend to the house so they could play together. To Stella's surprise, one day a young boy knocked on the door asking to speak with Esy.

"I'm Moyo. Is Esy here?"

"Hello young man, please come in."

Moyo walked through the front door with his eyes staring at the floor. He entered haltingly. He needed more encouragement from Stella.

"Come on in, Moyo. How do you know Esy?" Stella asked.

"Esy is my sister," he said in barely a whisper.

"I didn't know she had a brother. How did you find my house?"

"Asha gave me a slip of paper with your address written on it.

"Who is Asha?

Moyo stopped speaking and just stood there, refusing to answer any more questions. He waited for his sister.

"Esy, a boy named Moyo is here to see you," Stella shouted down the stairs.

"My brother has come to see me! Wonderful!" Esy said, as she skipped up the steps. "So good to see you," she said as she wrapped her arms around him and held him for a long time. When she stood back and looked at him, Moyo seemed much older. His expression was less child-like, more withdrawn than it had been before.

Esy tried to think of something that would make Moyo feel less awkward. "Do you want to play soccer in the backyard?" she asked.

"Yes," Moyo said, his face brightening.

"Come on. Let me show you the way. We can talk and play at the same time."

Esy could see that Moyo was uneasy in Stella's nice house. She was right to suggest playing in the backyard.

"How did you find this place?" Moyo asked.

"It's a long story, but this is the same house where Mama lived with Amelia and Bertrand. Mama wrote the address of the house in her journal. I knocked on the door and asked for Amelia and Bertrand's address."

"Are you their servant?"

"Yes, I am their servant. I cook supper and do some cleaning, but they want me to study hard so I do well in school. So far, it's working out well."

"You're going to school?"

"Yes I am, and I enjoy it so much. Once I find a way, I'll make sure you can go to school too."

"Mama would be happy."

"How is your work?"

"Hard. I cough a lot there, my lungs hurt most days."

"Do you have to give your money to Daddy?"

"Yes, I pay him every day."

"Ask him to bring you to the clinic. A doctor there will give you some medicine."

"He always seems like he's too busy."

"Tell him that I told you to get help."

"I will."

"Where do you stay?" Esy asked.

"I stay with a family that lives near the mine. They have two sons that work there, and we walk to work together in the morning and after work."

"Do they treat you well?"

"Yes, they take care of me like I'm family. I've never been away this long, so I better get home or they'll worry about me."

"I'm so glad you came to see me. Come again, okay?"

"I will."

They hugged good-bye and then, walked around the house. Esy watched her brother go off down the road growing smaller with every step. As he disappeared out of sight, her heart ached because she knew her brother did grueling work. She was resolved to help Moyo find a better life. If there was a way to help she would, but she had to make her efforts at school pay off first. Inside she raged at her father for being so selfish and uncaring about his son. *Is he not able to see how much Moyo needs him? Is gambling more important than his children? His mind is consumed by getting money and he's oblivious to the pain and anguish he's causing by his driving need to win big. Winning big is losing big for his children. I've been given a chance to climb out of that hole, but Moyo hasn't. Mama was destroyed by Daddy's selfishness. I'd like to shake him out of his foolishness.*

ରେ ରେ ରେ

After her brother left, Patch and Esy let off steam. They romped together, running around the house playing peek-a-boo. Esy giggled as Patch made quick turns, swished her tail and eluded her grasp around the corners. After Esy prepared dinner, there was about a half-hour when pandemonium reigned in the home. Often, Russell would be playful when he got home from the mine, so the two of them would play soccer and a rousing game of tag. When the play was up, Russell would tickle Esy signaling that playtime was over. It was a giggle fest for her but, for Russell, there was more to it—Esy sensed his attraction to her.

The more Russell enjoyed his home life, the less frequent were his "business" trips. The dinners Esy made were the African meals her mother taught her, but Stella had an occasional hankering for European food. She would buy the ingredients and leave a new recipe on the counter. Esy enjoyed making different food because it was like going to cooking school. She liked the challenge even though some of those meals were flops—for example, her Yorkshire pudding was a sloppy mess.

At twelve years of age going on thirteen, Esy started to mature. The first signs were the budding of her breasts, the growth of pubic hair, and the start of her periods. Esy was mostly awkward and shy about all these changes. When men looked her way, she smiled demurely and looked down. She wasn't aware that she was becoming a beautiful and an appealing young lady—education was more important. Her features were symmetrical and strong. Her eyes were a melt-your-heart chocolate brown and her dark smooth skin framed a disarmingly white smile. Esy's body was athletic and her elegant posture gave her a hint of nobility.

CRCRCR

Despite the pleasure Stella derived from Esy's presence, she still had an inexhaustible yearning for a baby. Somehow, having Esy as a substitute daughter just wasn't enough. Day and night the feelings of her barrenness haunted her. She questioned why she had to suffer such emptiness. She became obsessed by a dark wish. This secret lurked inside of her and created intense shame. The angst of hiding it, made it grow like cancer. Finally, after harboring this hidden desire for almost a year, Stella was driven to act on it. She devised a way to implement her desire to have a baby hoping to free herself from the anguish. She approached Esy.

"Esy," she said. "Have you ever thought about having a family?"

"Oh, yes. That's a dream of mine."

"I think your body is ready."

"Ready for what?"

"To have a baby."

"I'm *not* ready to take care of a baby," Esy remarked.

"You wouldn't have to. I would take care of it."

Esy stood there in silence, eyes wide open until finally, she turned around and went downstairs. *What is Stella thinking? How would I have a baby and with what person? I just don't understand. Stella can be so peculiar sometimes. I want to finish my education before I have a family. Does she have a boy for me that I don't know about? Why would she want to take care of my baby? It just doesn't make sense. I know Stella has been sad about not being able to have her own baby, but making me have a baby is wrong for both Kimbanquists and Catholics. It's not like her to joke around—but maybe she's just trying to be funny. At school, the boys flirt with me sometimes and I feel so uneasy. It's not in my nature to want a boyfriend because I have to finish my studies.*

Russell came home at the usual time, but Esy didn't want to play. Her conversation with Stella was too confusing. Esy made dinner like she usually did, but she didn't want to play or eat. Instead, she wanted to be by herself. Fearing she might anger Stella, she hid in her room.

෬෬෬

"Hi, lover boy," Stella simpered when Russell came home. "Did you have a good day?" She leaned forward and kissed him.

"I can tell you want something. I know you *too* well, so, out with it."

"Esy is ready to have babies," Stella said with a glint in her eye. "She's menstruating."

"So?" Russell said, as he stepped away from her. "What does that have to do with *me?*"

"Please, sweetheart, just hear me out," Stella said, producing soulful tears. "You know I've wanted a baby for a very long time. I feel so sad that I can't have one. Other women think I'm a failure as a woman."

"Stella—"

"This would make me *so* happy. If you would make her pregnant, I would love the baby and take care of it."

"Wow ... You've got to be crazy."

"No, I'm not crazy, I just want to find a way to free myself from being depressed. I want a baby to love so much. I know I would be a good mother and you would be a good father."

I'll have to give this some thought," Russell said.

It was silent in the Cox household. The tension in the air was *anything* but usual, and Russell looked at Esy with a different kind of intensity.

CRCRCR

In the following weeks, a new after dinner ritual started. Russell and Esy would go for a ride in his car to get ice cream. They giggled and laughed as they tried out different flavors and enjoyed the night air. They would pop the top of the convertible and sit on the top of the back seat to watch the sun set. Each night the times together grew longer, and as time went on, the giggling stopped, leaving an uncertain silence.

At some point the uncertainty became acceptable. Esy would spend time alone replaying Stella's deepest desires—they seemed almost normal. Deep down inside was an ache persuading her to please Stella and make her happy. Esy suspected that Russell had that same ache. It was something neither one of them could dismiss. Stella made cookies for her, paid for school supplies, celebrated her one-hundred percents, and in many ways, was her mother substitute. When Stella was depressed, it affected everyone in the house. Her pleasant features would look old and haggard. Stella was sinking fast and the only activity that pulled out of the hole was planning for a baby. Just the thought of that changed her outlook. Her posture became stronger and there was a playful glint in her eyes.

When she reflected honestly, Esy began to be hopeful that having Russell's baby would cement her place in the Cox family. With her mother gone and her father a wastrel, she was essentially an orphan. Completing an education was her fervent goal, but her relationships seemed uncertain and lacking. She wanted to belong somewhere.

The outings after supper for ice cream and a ride in the car became routine. One especially beautiful night as darkness surrounded them, Russell's arm slipped around Esy's waist. He pulled her close and kissed her, his lips warm and seeking hers, sending tingles through her body. With Stella's campaign in mind, after many nights together, he brought her to a fancy hotel room with dim, intimate lighting. Russell caressed her until she yielded. She so wanted to please Russell and make Stella happy.

∽∽∽

Esy carried the baby very high since nature and her natural athleticism blessed her young body with strong abdominal muscles. Each day she went to school to learn as much as she could before the school year ended and before her pregnancy was obvious. Esy was still an outsider in her school, so she didn't know if anyone noticed her bump. She slid past some girls who would meet in small groups and laugh as she walked by. They never said to anything to her, so Esy was unfazed and went about her solitary way.

In her bedroom when the day was spent, Esy would think about her future. *What will this baby be like? The baby will have two mothers and one father. How will that work out? Do the girls at school know I'm pregnant? Will Stella take good care of the baby?*

Esy noticed that once she became pregnant, Russell didn't take her in his car to get ice cream any more. This made her think about the time when she was a little girl and she heard her mother mention that when she was pregnant with Moyo, Daddy Dayana wasn't interested in her any more. Esy concluded that this was the same for Russell and perhaps, for most men. This didn't bother her because her schoolwork kept her busy enough. Completing her education continued to be her main focus.

Besides the pregnancy being constantly on her mind, Esy was aware of consequential events happening in the Belgian Congo. One day, Esy's history teacher, Mr. Muamba, burst into class carrying a transistor radio. He was excited to announce Congo's independence from Belgium, marking the end of colonial rule. It was a Friday, the morning after the 30th of June, 1960. He informed the class about the ceremony that had been held at the Palais National, the previous governor general's residence. He indicated that building would become the symbol of the new government, and house its parliament. He shared what he knew about the ceremony to a rapt group of students. As protocol would dictate, the newly elected Prime Minister Lumumba came in first followed by King Baudouin from Belgium and finally, President Kassavubu. The audience stood to honor and greet the King and the new President. After all the unrest in the country, Mr. Muamba was surprised by the peaceful nature of the transition. He turned the radio on for the class so they could hear the radio announcer in French repeating the words of President Kassavubu:

"Ladies and gentlemen, you have heard the speech given by His Majesty, the King of Belgium. As from this moment on, Congo is independent."

The class went crazy, hugging each other, jumping up and down and dancing. They didn't know that what would follow would be chaotic lawlessness caused by a corrupt legacy and the birth of a new nation. Esy was eager to talk to Stella and Russell about the huge shift in power and wondered how the change would affect Russell's job.

ଌଔଌ

Esy had a plan for her life. If all went well, she would have Russell and Stella's baby during summer break in December. Chances are that her teachers and fellow students would not notice her pregnancy if she kept out of the spotlight and wore her uniform in a certain way. Once the baby was born, Stella would assume its care. School would start again after a six-week break in mid-January, and she would continue her schooling as if nothing had happened. A baby in the house would make Stella happy. Russell would be happy because Stella was happy, and Esy would be happy because there would be no interruptions in her education.

She could feel the baby kicking when she rested on her bed. It was exciting and she chose to share it with Stella. They both giggled about how the baby kicked at the end of the day when she was trying to rest after school.

"I think he wants me to keep moving—he likes the rocking motion when I walk," Esy said, as she saw Stella's eyes becoming bright with anticipation.

Depression at the Cox home had lifted and it was a joy to be part of the family again. Joyful anticipation prevailed.

Esy was delighted because of her country's new independence, which was something Mama Mary had desired. Anticipation was part of her life—anticipation for her new baby and for the birth of a new country. Esy was certain that changing cities to African names would happen in her lifetime. She would give her baby an African name, too and that would make Mama proud. Leopoldville, the capital of the Belgium Congo, would be renamed, "Congo-Kinshasha," according to popular opinion. Esy was excited and optimistic about her future and her baby's future.

ও ও ও

One day during history class, Mr. Muamba discussed in great detail the events that led up to independence. This discourse was anything but optimistic. From 1955 to 1960 the movement toward independence went lightening quick. Not just one man, but many men stirred the "political stew" that spearheaded this high-speed road to decolonization. These operatives were constantly on the move. This political game according to David Van Reybrouck in his book, *Congo, The Epic History of a People* was like a fast game of Ping-Pong with many players and numerous balls. Slams, tricky volleys and sleight of hand movements created sudden shifts of power overwhelming the Congolese people. Most of the maneuvers were in the heavily populated cities, which made it difficult to incorporate the myriad of different cultures. Many tribes lived deep in the forests or on the grasslands by the Congo River. They were unaware of the major transitions of power.

Mr. Muamba expounded on another event, which had a direct impact on Russell's job. On June 27, 1960, three days before independence, the Belgian parliament disbanded the Comité Special du Katanga, this was part of the Anglo-Belgian Mining Company. Knowing that Katanga Province was planning to secede from the new government, this company put all their owed taxes in Tshomba's bank account, which funded the secession from the First Republic of the Congo. The Congolese government, in power at the time, unwittingly sanctioned this action. Unfortunately, the First Republic lost out on the millions of dollars of taxes from the Comité Special du Katanga. Without this income, it was very difficult for the First Republic to prosper. From this lack of foresight, the secession of the Katanga province was imminent. Mr Muamba explained the disastrous effect this had on the future of the First Republic of the Congo and on its economy.

Esy soon discovered from dinner conversations at the Cox residence that this agreement actually secured Russell's job. The relationship between Belgium and the mines in the Katanga province was strengthened, securing the European involvement in the Congolese economy.

CHAPTER 6

Running Away...

ᘓᘓᘓ

Esy gave birth to a baby boy. With his unusual combination of features, he was a marked child, an easy target for teasers and cynics. His dark skin was smooth and creamy, only one shade lighter than his mother's, his eyes an azure blue, and during his early childhood, he grew a shock of red hair. Within the Cox household, however, the baby was a loved darling. Stella fawned over Esy as she recovered from giving birth, and it was especially fun for her to have an infant in the house. Esy called him her little baby moon because of his round face. This prompted the name Mwezi, which means moon in Swahili. Mwezi smiled early and cuddled cutely in their arms. When wide awake, he joyfully bounced from Stella to Esy to Russell and back to Stella, and then, the musical chairs would start all over again. Even changing diapers was fun—they made a game of it. Stella recalled ditties from her childhood to sing to him; he smiled, laughed and cooed in appreciation.

When Mwezi cried, Russell did not know what to do. Stella, however, went down the list: Is his diaper wet or dirty? Does he need milk or want to be held? Does he need to be burped or does he have gas? Stella seemed to know intuitively what he needed at every moment—like she had a built in homing device.

The baby filled the little yellow house with the kind of laughter it had never known before. Russell stayed home and traveled less, reveling in his wife's happiness. Esy studied hard at school so she could make her life better and provide a promising future for her son. Everything seemed to be going well at the Cox household.

But gradually, things began to deteriorate. Russell began to prefer spending time Esy, and would draw her into clandestine trysts. On some days, he rendezvoused with her after school taking her out for an early ice cream or lured her into a store to buy lingerie.

It didn't take Stella long to figure out something was going on between them, and this discovery precipitated a jealous rage that mushroomed into anger the likes of which Russell had never known. She didn't want Russell to walk out on her, so Esy became the target of her wrath.

Between the pressures of taking care of Mwezi and being subjected to Stella's rants, Esy's schoolwork began to suffer. The once happy home unraveled and chaos ensued. Stella refused to take care of Mwezi and forced Esy to take care of him in her basement bedroom. On some nights, Esy's little moon-faced boy cried all night. Esy couldn't help but think he missed Stella, who used to dote on him so much. Esy was beside herself, not knowing what to do. And because Stella no longer wanted to look after Mwezi,

Esy had to strap him on her back in a kanga and head off to school. She tried to shush him during class time, but he would have none of it. His blues eyes would peek out at the students and they laughed and played with him. It disrupted her teachers and their lectures.

One day, Mr. Labon, the Director of the school, called Esy into his office and in no uncertain terms ordered Esy *not* to bring her baby to school again.

Crestfallen, Esy tried to make sense of her sudden reversal of fortune. *I can't stay with Stella and Russell and I can't bring Mwezi to school with me and I don't know anyone who would take care of him. I have no money for our future.* With few options open to her, and knowing that the only way she could earn enough money to care for Mwezi was to mine cobalt, Esy decided to run away and go back to mining. As much as she hated that work, she knew it was her only option.

Where will I live? Who would accept Mwezi? The first place she thought of was the mission near the Etoile mine. It was like her second home. She felt loved and accepted by Asha, Mary Ann, and David. So Esy strapped Mwezi in a kanga on her back and set out to visit them. With each step, she tried to understand the changes in her life. It all happened so fast. Finishing school seemed like a disappearing dream. She realized that now, her little moon-faced boy had to be her main focus and responsibility. Esy was prepared to love her son like her mama loved her.

As she approached the mission station, she recalled the last time she'd been there, and the narrow escape from Hackett Salomon and the uneasy encounter with her father. She remembered the night she spent in the burn barrel. She had made it back to the mission exhausted from the scary pursuit, and curled up in that very chair she saw on the porch. Asha had found her there and helped her out. She was so grateful for the help of all her friends.

By the time Esy reached the station, the mineworkers had left for their work in the mine, so she knocked on David's door hoping he would be in his office.

"Well, well. What a surprise! I've missed you. How are you doing?"

"I've had better times," Esy said. Mwezi started to cry.

"Who's that?"

"I never told you, but I had a baby boy, three months ago."

"Hi, cute little fella," David cooed. "But, Esy you're too young to have a baby. Who's the father?"

"Russell Cox."

"Isn't that the man whose home you're staying at in Elisabethville?"

"Yes, but I ran away. Stella got angry and mean."

David was quiet and thoughtful for a while. Then he said, "Russell must accept some responsibility for the baby. You shouldn't have to support him entirely by yourself. Fathers have to help." Then he smiled. "What's your baby's name?"

"Mwezi," Esy said as she bounced him on her knee. "I plan to talk to Russell later, but right now I need a safe place to stay with my boy. I'm going back to the mine to earn some money."

"Make sure Russell completes the paperwork stating that he is the Father. That will make Mwezi a Belgian citizen and will give him more opportunities. And, of course, you and Mwezi can stay here as long as you need to, but Mary Ann and I are so busy with the mission that we won't be able to take care of Mwezi." He led the two of them out of his office and showed them an empty room that was small but clean.

"Thank you for giving us a place to stay."

Esy busily organized the room, placed the two beds side-by-side, and opened up the window cloths to bring in the fresh air. This little room would be just fine for the two of them. Mwezi was wide-eyed, taking in all the sights and sounds as he clung to his mother while riding on her hip. Esy had taken three cloth diapers and two bottles from the Cox household before she left. She would use one of the diapers during the night, so she could sleep, and during the day while she worked in the mine. Then, she would have to hand wash the soiled one and let it air dry in the window. This motivated her to start toilet training. Mothers of new babies at the mission talked about the "elimination communication," a technique, which relied on a trusted communication arrangement between mother and child. This was used mostly in Africa.

"hissssss," she said to Mwezi and then, she took off his diaper and had him go. Her plan was to use this sound each time he went to the toilet, so he would pair the sound with elimination. Esy saw other African women's success with this technique, so she was determined to make this work for the two of them. At some point, Mwezi would say "hisssssss," which would indicate he had to go. She had to stay consistent.

Before the upheaval in the little yellow house, Stella would feed him while she was at school, but now, it was Esy's job. She retrieved milk from the kitchen and used the bottles at first. Then, she mashed bananas to start him on solid foods. He had a good appetite–his face lit up when he saw food. It was during feeding time that he began to really smile, which made Esy's heart melt. Undeniably, she loved her little moon-faced boy.

The next morning after eating, Esy strapped Mwezi on her back in a kanga, and made her way to the Etoile mine. All day in the hot sun, she labored to separate the cobalt from the copper and nickel. Mwezi fell asleep in his kanga and the hot sun made him lethargic. Occasionally, Esy would feed him a bottle of water or milk, and she would dig a hole in the red dirt and say "hisssssss," and sometimes he would go. Of course she would praise and cuddle him—this was all part of the training. After feeding time, the movements of his mother's body rocked Mwezi back to sleep. As the sun set behind the horizon, Esy and Mwezi headed back to the mission station, hungry and tired. *I hope Asha is there so we can catch up on our lives. I'm surprised I didn't see her at the mine today.* Esy looked for her friend, but she was nowhere to be found. Mary Ann was in the kitchen, so she asked her about Asha.

"Asha isn't here any longer. We just found out that she's at the Ruashi mine," Mary Ann said.

"Oh, no," Esy said. "Why did she go there?"

"Hackett Salomon said he needed her at that mine. She comes here to visit whenever she can, so we see her often. I'm sure she'll be here tomorrow night."

"I miss her so much."

"David said you have a little boy."

"Yes, he's asleep right now, but I'll bring him down for supper."

"I like to hold babies."

Esy went back to her room to a fussy baby. She had a

little milk left in the bottle, so she fed it to him. When finished she took him to the bathroom and said,"hisssssss." Mwezi went. *I like this. It is working!* She washed out the diaper he had on and let it dry in the windowsill overnight. She put the dry one on him and went to supper. Esy was starving from working all day, and they had her favorite meal, salt fish and cassava leaves. The fun-loving Esy was more subdued since her younger days at the mission house. She didn't join in the laughter and didn't participate in the soccer games. Mary Ann and Esy took care of and played with Mwezi instead. Esy knew it was her job as a mother.

Esy tucked her baby close to her in her bed. They kept each other warm in the cool of the night. The next morning would be another workday. She would place Mwezi in a kanga, strap him to her back, and trudge to the mine. This became the routine without fail for two weeks.

The beginning of the third week, Mwezi became very ill. He coughed until he became weak. He was feverish, lost his appetite, and became limp. Esy panicked and went to Mary Ann for help. She welcomed the older woman's wisdom and followed her advice to the letter. Esy held Mwezi close, rocked him, and wiped his little brow with a moist cloth making sure he had water and good food. After a week of recovery, he regained his health. She strapped him in the kanga on her back and went to work in the mine again.

Esy discovered an area in the crags of the mine that had an excellent stockpile of cobalt. This find proved to be profitable for her. She worked feverishly, adding to her stash, and was paid handsomely by the Chinese broker at the end of the day. But Mwezi developed a cough again, and would gasp for air, especially in the evening. There was a pattern starting. It seemed that Mwezi became sick after two weeks in the mine. Once again, she nurtured him back to health. Having made some money at the mine, she decided to bring her son to a doctor to get some answers. She would have to go to the clinic in Elisabethville. It was hard to get appointments at the clinic because you had to wait until you could get in. So it took a couple of days for a doctor to see Mwezi. She waited patiently outside the clinic. Fortunately, the third day Dr. Raingeard was on duty. He did some preliminary tests and found those to be unremarkable. However, he took a long time listening to Mwezi's lungs. When he looked up, he shook his head.

"His lungs are weak and raspy. I've heard that type of lung sound in children who have worked in the mines for a long time. They're allergic to the cobalt dust."

"Mwezi, allergic to the cobalt dust?" Esy said. "I have been strapping him on my back while I work at the mine," Esy said, "I have to work there because I need the money. How can I help him feel better?"

"It is certain that the dust in the mine is making him sick," Dr. Raingeard said. "I have some medicine I'll send home with you. Give it to him three times a day. This should keep his lungs healthy."

"Is there anything else I can do?"

"Have him wear a mask or a kerchief on his face to keep the dust away from his nose. Also, you need to find some *other* kind of work to support the two of you."

"I'll do my best. Thank you, Doctor."

I don't know what to do. Mwezi has to be with me when I work. I don't know anyone who will take care of him. Esy's hike back to the mission was a lonely one. She hoped so much that Asha would stop by for a visit so she could talk to her. Esy said a prayer hoping God would hear the concern she had for her son. She knew working in the mine was her only choice for a while, and she had to keep Mwezi strapped on her back while she worked. Esy hoped the medication for the dust would keep him healthy, at least, for a while.

As she approached the mission station, she looked for signs of Asha, but there were none. She saw Mary Ann rocking on the porch, her eyes downcast.

"Hi, Mary Ann. How are you?"

"Oh, I'm worrying," she said as she looked up. "David wants to find Asha since she hasn't been back to visit for over a week."

"She's working at the Ruashi mine, right?" Esy asked.

"The last time we spoke to her, that's where she was working. But as I said, it's been over a week, and that's not like Asha."

"I'm going there. To the Ruashi mine."

"When?"

"Right now."

"I can watch Mwezi for you so you don't have to carry him on your back," Mary Ann graciously offered. "He's such a cute little fella."

"Thank you, Mary Ann," Esy said. "That will make the trip easier. His bottle and diaper are on the shelf in our room."

Esy started the long journey to the Ruashi mine late in the day, which meant that much of the trip would be in the dark after sunset. She walked quickly until she was too tired to keep going and found some soft grass under a tree, where she slept until morning. When she woke up to the sound of children's voices, Esy knew the mine-workers had started their journey to the mine. *I hope I hear Asha's voice among the chatter.*

Esy stood and looked at the children going to the mine, but Asha was not among them. *Where is my friend?*

Esy looked everywhere she could think of, behind every mound and hill at the Ruashi mine. While stand-ing on the ridge— her old work territory—she felt an eerie presence. She whirled around, and found herself looking straight at the ample chest of Hackett Salomon. She looked up into his smug eyes.

"Where is my friend Asha?"

"Why do you want to know?" he asked. His eyes narrowed.

"I want to find out how she's doing."

"She's living in a house in Elisabethville just a couple doors down from Viktor von Peeters."

"Why is she there?"

"I'll let her speak for herself," Hackett said, as his lips formed a devious smile.

Esy set out to backtrack over the same road she'd come by in the scorching midday sun. Knowing she would be thirsty, she drank her fill of water at the mining camp before she left.

Esy walked as quickly as she could to Elizabethville to see her friend. *Why is Asha living near Viktor von Peeters? My worst fears are that she has become part of Viktor and Hackett's schemes and trickery.*

As she passed the little white house where she escaped the clutches of Hackett Salomon's henchmen by a hair's breadth, Esy shivered. Two doors down was another little house with a red door where her friend lived. With trepidation, Esy knocked. When the door opened, she jumped back in astonishment. "Asha! Is that you?"

The girl in front of her looked like Asha, but she was wearing fancy new clothes and glittering jewelry. Her hair was cut in a cute style and her lips were a bright red.

"Hi Esy. You look surprised," Asha smiled.

"It's just...you look so different. What's going on? Where did you get these clothes?"

"These?" Asha spread her arms and turned in a circle. "Hilda, our housemother buys the clothes for me when she shops in Elisabethville. Do you like the colors?" The bright full-length caftan was eye-catching, almost over-whelming. A shiny, sequined black edging outlined neon pink and chartreuse stripes. Her gold earrings hung down so low they almost touched her shoulders. This was so different from the dark blue dresses the two of them were accustomed to wearing while they worked in the mine.

The woman Asha introduced as Hilda was cooking lunch in the kitchen. The food smelled good and Esy was hungry. Her stomach growled out loud.

"Would you like to have lunch with us?" Asha asked.

"Yes, please."

"Hilda, please set another plate for my friend."

Lunch was full of surprises. Asha explained what she did, and it made Esy blush. She couldn't bring herself to make eye contact with Asha or Hilda. Doing this kind of work, being with men for money, was something shame-ful.

Yet to Esy's surprise, Asha appeared happy and well fed. It all looked so easy. After they finished lunch, Asha gave her a tour of the two-story house. Her bedroom on the ground floor was simple and clean, with a lovely pink bed cover. There was a bathroom too, just like Esy's old room at Stella's house. Down the hallway there was another bedroom near Asha's that was empty.

"Hackett is looking for another girl for this room," Asha said as she looked at Esy.

"What's upstairs?" Esy asked.

"That's where we see the men, no one else is allowed in those bedrooms."

Esy remained quiet for a long time. "Who are these men?"

"They are men I've never met before," Asha said. "Some are the Chinese brokers from the market, others from Europe, or men from the village of Elisabethville. Last night I was with a scientist from Russia."

"What do you do with them?" Esy asked after another long pause.

"I mostly listen to what they have to say. If they want sexual favors, I do what they ask. It's pretty easy. They give Hilda a lot of money."

"Do you get money?"

"Yes, I get a certain amount for every man I see and I keep the tips they leave."

"There is something that I haven't told you about," Esy said sheepishly.

"What's that?"

"I have a little baby boy."

"You what! You have a baby? Why didn't you tell me that before?"

"I've been looking for you. I waited for you at the mission station because Mary Ann said you visit there often. I walked to the Ruashi mine to find you, and I ran into Hackett Salomon. He told me where you were. I've missed you so much."

"I thought you were still living with Stella and Russell. What happened?"

Esy filled Asha in on all that had happened since the two friends last saw each other. "Now, David and Mary Ann let me stay at the mission station with Mwezi when I work in the mine," Esy said.

"They are good people," Asha exclaimed.

"Mary Ann is taking care of Mwezi right now. It made the journey easier when I walked to the Ruashi mine to look for you. I needed to find you so we could talk."

"Oh, Esy. I'm so glad you came," Asha said, as she tearfully hugged her friend. Silence followed their long embrace.

"I have another problem. Mwezi's lungs are weak and the doctor thinks it's because the air in the mine is bad for him. He told me to find some other work."

"Do you want to do what I'm doing?" Asha asked.

"I didn't think I wanted to before, but Mwezi's condition is making me rethink everything."

"I can talk to Hilda and she can run it by Hackett."-

"Who would take care of Mwezi?"

"Oh, that might be a problem," Asha responded. "Let me talk to Hilda first, and then I'll come to visit you at the mission station tomorrow."

"I'll see you soon."

How did my life get so complicated? Now, I have someone beside myself to feed and keep safe. This changes everything. I want the best life possible for Mwezi, so I might have to do a job I don't find respectable.

Esy found motherhood so perplexing. She loved and missed Mwezi so much even though she knew Mary Ann would give him the best care. After all, it had only been a day. *Did she use the toileting communication with him? Did he get his bottle and food at the right time? Did he miss me?*

As she approached the mission station, Esy saw Mary Ann and Mwezi peering out the front window. When Mwezi saw Esy, he squealed with delight. She broke into a happy run. Hugs and laughter followed, and Esy was certain that motherhood was the best job she could ever have.

"Thank you for watching Mwezi. Was he a good boy?"

"He is a sweet boy. You're a very lucky Mama," Mary Ann replied.

"Asha said she would come for a visit tomorrow. She wants to meet Mwezi, and have lunch with us."

"I've missed her, so I'll prepare something special for our time together," Mary Ann said.

Esy carried Mwezi to their room. She fed and bathed him and then, they napped together. She knew that Mary Ann would not approve of servicing men for a job, so she stayed quiet, and chose not to create controversy. Besides, Esy was not even sure that it would all work out. Tomorrow Asha would have news to share about her conversation with Hilda.

CR CR CR

As Esy was busying herself with Mwezi's care, there was a knock on the door. She knew it was Asha.

"Come in, my friend."

She opened the door to an exuberant young lady she hardly recognized as Asha. She was wearing another lovely caftan in muted, sophisticated colors. The same long gold earrings dangled just above her shoulders.

"Who is this cute little boy?" Asha asked.

"This is my son, Mwezi."

Mwezi put his head shyly on his mama's shoulder and peeked at their visitor. Asha laughed and played peek-a-boo with him.

"So adorable," she said. "How old is he?"

"He's six months old. My life has never been the same. He brings me so much joy."

"I have more good news," Asha said. "Hilda talked to Hackett. Both of them would welcome you and Mwezi to our house in Elisabethville."

"Did they say anything else?" Esy asked.

"Like how you would earn your keep?"

"Yes."

"You would be servicing men in the evening like I do."

Esy did not know how to feel, happy or miserable. She just couldn't decide, although she was certain of one emotion—relieved that Mwezi would not have to go to the mine with her any more. Her deepest hope was that his lungs would heal. Even at her age, Esy knew that life would be hard and that doing what she had to do to secure a better future for her son might be brutal at times. She vowed to give Mwezi an excellent education to give him every chance to make his dreams come true—whatever they turned out to be.

"Who would take care of Mwezi when I'm doing this?"

"Hilda said she would take care of him," Asha said. "She was worried that he might cry when the men were upstairs. That is something that would be bad for business, so you might have to take him out of the house, but she was sure something could be worked out."

"Where would I take him?"

"I don't know. That's something you need to ask Hilda," Asha said.

"When do you want me to come to live with you?"

"As soon as you can. There is an empty room waiting for you."

"Mwezi and I will be there tomorrow," Esy said. "Mary Ann prepared a special lunch for you, so we need to get to the dining room."

Delicious smells emanated from the that room. It was the smell of fresh fish fried in butter and Jollof rice stir-fried with onions, peppers, and tomatoes. All cooked to perfection. The dessert was a special seasonal treat of freshly picked and sliced mangoes.

"Asante," Asha said, touched by the effort Mary Ann had made for her.

"And thank you to you too. I'm so happy you came for a visit," Mary Ann responded with a smile.

The next day, Esy packed up her few possessions, said good-bye to Mary Ann, and started her walk to Elisabethville with her son strapped on her back.

"Well, Mwezi, I don't know what will happen next, but we are in this together. I love you so much and I know we will find a way for both of us to have a happy life."

Esy reached behind her and tickled his little baby feet through the holes in the kanga.

"ollumcee," he cooed.

His baby talk was so expressive and that made her proud. He seemed to be verbal and bright. Mwezi had just started to laugh out loud, which made the trip go faster with their antiphony of giggles. In spite of the family calamity at Stella and Russell's home, the bond between mother and child stayed viable and strong. The two of them had forged a relationship that would conquer any ill-fated encounters.

∽∾∽∾∽

Esy decided to treat her new job as an adventure and an eye-opening learning experience. This would be much better for her son and as soon as she gathered enough courage, she would ask Hilda how much money she would make. Her plan was to save as much as possible for schooling and for medical expenses.

Hilda opened the front door soon after she knocked.

"Hello, Esy. I've been waiting for you. Glad you came today so we can get some things done before I have my day off," Hilda said. "My, my. What have we here?" Hilda helped Esy untie the kanga and lifted Mwezi into her arms. "It has been a while since I've had a little one. He is a cute one and I think he has two dimples. I've heard that babies with dimples are kissed by an angel before they leave heaven to visit earth."

"Really?" Esy said, smiling. Hilda appeared to have a nice way with children, and Esy hoped that meant she could trust her with Mwezi. "Do you have children?"

"Yes, I have three, but they're all grown up," Hilda said. "Let me show you your room."

Esy and Mwezi followed her through a hallway to a bright, clean room. There were two beds with mattresses, a high bed for Esy and one on the floor for Mwezi.

"This one would be safer for your little boy. When he starts to get active, he'll roll on the floor from the low mattress, and he won't get hurt."

"I like this room very much. Thank you, Hilda," Esy said. "I have some questions about my job."

"Ask anything, and I'll try to give you an answer."

"How do I act when I'm servicing the men?"

"First of all, you won't be servicing the men for at least a couple of months. We have to make sure your body is clean and free of any diseases. We'll pamper you, re-style your appearance, and train you to follow certain routines to please the men you serve. So relax, be patient, and your questions will be answered."

"How much do I get paid?"

"It varies so much that it's hard to give you an answer. The fee for the men is fifty francs, but usually they tip very well. All the tips are yours and you get a certain percentage of the fee the men pay. The percentage you get is Hackett's decision. Does that answer your question?"

"Yes."

"One more important detail. Asha is servicing men tonight and Mwezi needs to be very quiet. Baby sounds would disturb the men, something we do not want," Hilda said.

"What do I do if he cries?"

"Take him outside immediately and walk away from the house to stay out of hearing range," Hilda said. "I'll be here tonight, so I can help if you need me."

"Do you want me to make meals?"

"I will make dinner for you, Mwezi, and Asha. It's important that you have a good dinner because you'll need lots of energy for your evenings with the men. You're on your own for breakfast and lunch, however. I'll buy groceries, so leave me a list of what you and Mwezi will need."

"Do you want me to make a list tonight?"

"Yes, tomorrow your program will start right after breakfast, so you won't have a lot of time. Asha said she would take care of your son while you're in training.

Knock on my door if you need help with Mwezi. We do *not* want the men to hear a baby cry. Do you have any more questions?"

"I can't think of any right now."

"Until tomorrow then, goodnight." Hilda walked to her bedroom on the other side of the house.

Esy went back to her room to find her baby sleeping. This usually meant that he would wake up in the middle of the night wanting to snuggle, eat, and play. She prepared his bottle, took out the clean diaper, and tried to sleep. Three hours later, Mwezi awoke as she predicted he would, ready to eat and play. After a long, exasperated sigh, she changed his diaper, fed him his bottle, and rocked him. She heard muffled noises upstairs and dreaded the necessity of taking Mwezi outside if he cried or wanted to vocalize. With his bottle done, Mwezi wanted to play. Quietly, she packed up some toys, a diaper, and walked down the street in the middle of the night to a bench by a bus stop and played with her son until the man left about an hour later.

ରେ ରେ ରେ

The next morning came too soon. Mwezi was fast asleep, all the play tired him out. Esy fixed his morning bottle and placed a fresh diaper on the bed, and left the room to meet Hilda. Esy had mixed emotions about starting "the program." She reminded herself that this experience had changed Asha many ways for the better. *I wonder if it will change me? I hope it will turn out well.*

"Good morning, Esy," Hilda said. "How did it go last night?"

"About two in the morning, I took Mwezi to the bench

by the bus stop. He wanted to coo and play. Asha and the man were done about an hour later, so I came back and tried to get some sleep."

"Is your son sleeping, now?"

"Yes."

"Asha usually gets up about ten, so I'll have her watch Mwezi when she wakes up."

"That should work. I have everything ready for her," Esy said.

"Good. Are you ready for the program?" Hilda asked.

"I'm as ready as I can be."

"The first part involves cleansing. Hackett wants his houses to have a good reputation, which means they have in their houses ladies who are clean and genteel. You must drink some wormwood powder to rid yourself of any parasites you might have."

"I have *parasites?*" Esy asked, horrified.

"Probably. Many people have them from eating tainted meat, uncooked vegetables and tree fruit. It's pretty common," Hilda said, as she handed her the dreadful wormwood concoction. "You'll have to drink this for five days and then, you'll take five days off. The life cycle of the parasites necessitates that you drink it again every day for another five days and finally, that part of the program will be done. Once you've done, we're going to make those calloused feet soft with some scented oils."

Esy drank the bitter medicine, grimacing with each swallow. Gradually, taking one sip at a time, she finished it. Fifteen days of this would seem like a long time.

"Now it's time to massage your feet."

The smells emanating from the oils that Hilda was preparing were exquisite. It was a fragrance Esy had never smelled before, woody, warm, and spicy. "What is that smell?"

"I use Myrrh as my scent of choice for the feet. Do you like it?"

"Very much."

"Now, watch me when I do your feet. Some men want a foot massage, so after I do it for you, you'll know how to do it for them."

"Does this mean when my feet are soft, I'll have to wear shoes?"

"Yes," Hilda said, with a chuckle. "I'll buy some black, comfortable shoes for you to wear. It is important that you keep your feet smooth and clean at all times."

Down the hall, there were sounds of Asha and Mwezi singing and clapping their hands together. The mood changed quickly. Esy wanted to play with Mwezi.

"Well, that's enough for today," Hilda said. "Tomorrow I have the day off, so I plan to shop for your shoes. After breakfast, the next day, I'll have you give me a foot massage for practice. We'll find out how much you remember. In the meantime, if you have questions, write them down when you think of them."

After playing with Mwezi and Asha for a while, Esy made lunch for all of them. Mwezi went down for his nap, so Esy took some time to write out some questions for Hilda and Hackett. For Hilda, she asked questions about the services. What are the best oils to use for other massages? What smells would be best for the patrons' room? Would she be wearing caftans like Asha? Should she serve the men food? Who keeps the rooms clean? For Hackett her questions had to do with money. What percentage of the fee would she get? If she decided to leave this job, what would she need to do? If she or Mwezi became sick, how would the medical bills be paid? This was all new to her, and the unknown was disconcerting.

 catalog

The next two months flew by. Hilda had positive comments about Esy's ability to learn. She used oils daily to keep her feet soft, and accepted the constraints of her new black shoes. They were actually quite comfortable. During this time, Mwezi had become more mobile, crawling everywhere. By the end of the day, the little one was exhausted and slept through the night most of the time.

Mwezi was a ray of sunshine in the home. He loved to play with the kitchen pots and pans. He'd crawl over to the bottom kitchen drawers and pull them out one at a time. One time when Esy walked into the kitchen, she found him with a pan on his head banging it with a ladle.

"Oh, M you make me laugh," Esy chuckled.

From that day on, Mwezi was called M. It suited him because he filled the house with merriment, made everyone laugh, and often acted like a little monkey.

Esy enjoyed the first two training months. With all the good food and the oil massages, her skin became vibrant and she had boundless energy. Hilda answered most of her questions regarding the best fragrances. According to Hilda, lavender and myrrh were the best. Myrrh was intense and penetrating but lavender was soothing. When Esy asked what kind of clothes would be best for her, Hilda surprised her when she said she had beautiful athletic legs. That being so, short skirts and simple tops would suit her best. Her hair would be cropped and styled. Maybe she could wear some sassy bangs as her hair grew longer. Esy would look like a 1960s girl right out of the *Seventeen* magazines.

Getting Hackett to answer her questions or commit to a business arrangement was another story. He stopped by about halfway through her training and told Esy that she was becoming a beautiful young lady. When she asked about what percentage of the fee she would get, he just shrugged his shoulders.

"I am investing a lot of money in you," Hackett said. "We're buying food, clothes and some medicines for you. Your pay will depend on how much you please your clients. The more satisfied the men, the more money you make."

"What if I'm not a good fit for this job, what should I do?" Esy asked.

"Let's not think about that right now. You *will* be a good fit," Hackett said.

ൟൟൟ

Finally, it was time to begin. She prepared the room with lovely candles, the restful scent of lavender, and made sure the white sheets were clean. Heavy drapes at the windows and candlelight helped to create an intimate atmosphere suitable for quiet conversation and relaxing massages. There was a large bed in the center with two straight-back chairs along the walls. In the corner was a comfortable overstuffed chair.

Soon Esy would meet her first customer. She was a little nervous, but Hilda had trained her well. Poised to do her very best, she smiled, listened, listened and smiled, and massaged for long hours. She forgot herself and concentrated on the men's pleasure. It wasn't about her. What she was doing was about making money for M. Increasing savings for his future was of paramount importance. *He must have a better life than I do. He must become educated so he can have a happy life. This is my goal, and this goal will keep me focused.*

When both Esy and Asha were busy with customers, Hilda took care of M. Esy's son was a delightful child who relished the attention from all three ladies of the house. During the day, when Esy was trying to sleep, his antics would wake her. He would play peek-a-boo with her blankets and make her laugh or he would crawl under her bed and make baby noises. Each day with M was an adventure.

Esy's business clientele grew substantially. Each night new men were in her schedule. By word of mouth, men would seek out Esy since her services had a good reputation. For Esy some sessions were better than others, but generally, the men tipped her well, and she considered it a relatively easy way to make money. Esy learned how to be a servant and to do what the people around her wanted. She was trained well by her mother, Big Boss, and Stella how to be a good one. When she serviced the men, she learned to do what they wanted. Each customer wanted something different, so she had to be a good listener. Her life in the brothel became routine, like any other job. Her money was accumulating as she deposited her night earnings in the Belgian Central Bank of Elisabethville. This gave Esy satisfaction.

The bright spots in her day revolved around M. He walked early and by now, he had a walk-run. He was growing up so fast. His favorite pastime was playing peek-a-boo. He would hide behind a door and jump out with an "I see you" in baby talk and then, giggle. He loved Hilda's squeals, and M brought out her childish side. At times, they chased through the house like wild monkeys, carousing and teasing each other.

M's first words were mama, milk, ball and "igs," which was short for figs. He never knew a dada, so he had no reason to learn the word. M loved to eat and he cooed with delight when his meals included figs. The big red shock of hair grew longer and lovelier and was a painful reminder of Russell for Esy. As M became more mobile he was harder to handle and needed both Hilda and Asha to be his sitters while his mother worked. Nevertheless, he continued to bring mirth and merriment to the little white house in Elisabethville.

಄಄಄಄

Charles? Who is he? I've never worked for a Charles before. Esy figured it must be a new client and set about preparing her room with lavender and myrrh fragrances as usual. She made sure the sheets smelled fresh, and then placed everything neatly where it belonged. For her, order was the key to a peaceful environment. Esy gained a reputation for her good massages, careful listening, and sense of humor. The men left feeling rejuvenated. Esy glanced in the mirror to make sure her hair looked nice before answering the knock on the door.

"Hi, Esy," Russell said.

Shocked by the specter of Russell Cox, and upset that someone called her by name since she had tried to keep her real name a secret to her customers. "Russell!" she cried out. He was the last person she expected to see. Everything inside her head became blurry, her heart pounded in her chest, and she passed out, collapsing on the floor. She came to when Russell tried to revive her with a glass of cold water. As Esy regained consciousness, she chastised herself for her weak constitution.

"Don't worry about that," Russell said. "I understand your fear—and your surprise."

Comforted by his words, Esy thanked him, took the glass from his hand and finished drinking the water.

"Why did you come?" Esy asked.

"Stella and I want you to come back," Russell pleaded. "How have you been?" Silence followed.

"I consider myself lucky," she said after a long pause.

"You do?"

"I have a place to sleep and good food, and Mwezi doesn't get sick from the cobalt dust."

"How's our son?"

"He's a good and funny boy," Esy said smiling. "How's Stella?"

"Stella is not doing well—drinking and sleeping too much."

"I'm sorry."

"She misses you and Mwezi," Russell slumped, eyes downcast, so unlike his jovial manner in the past. "Would you please come back to live with us?"

Long silence. Esy's face became sullen and serious. Her eyes looked past him. There was so much she wanted to say to him, but her role as a servant girl made her stoic. Her feelings were so large inside, she had to go numb to stay in control.

"I promise you that I will never touch you that way again," Russell said.

"I don't know. I need to think about it for a long time."

After that painful reintroduction, the conversation changed to more mundane topics like the weather and the economy. Russell grew very quiet and then, began talking about the government. He had deep concerns about the violence that had erupted in the Congo following the murder of the first democratically elected Prime Minister, Patrice Lumumba. Esy listened intently, realizing how protected she was, how removed her life was from the melee of the militant people on the streets. With fear in his eyes, Russell abruptly stopped talking about politics.

"Please, put me in your schedule for next week," he said. "I need to talk to you again. I promise I will never touch you that way again."

Esy agreed and made an appointment for him the following week. He said good-bye and left her with the best tip she had ever received. She replayed the night over and over again, and contemplated his offer. *What would this mean for M? Would he like having a daddy? I wonder if Stella would be friendly or mean? Maybe Stella would revert back to her nasty side.* Esy had a lot to consider.

ʕ?ʕ?ʕ?

When Russell came the following week, the political situation was on his mind again. After Lumumba's demise, the officials of the Katanga Province where he worked rallied to support the secession of the province from the First Republic. The Katanga province mines were rich in nickel, copper, and cobalt and were self-sustaining. The province didn't need the constant threat of putsches, which is a quick and dirty overthrow of the government. There was talk of the Kasai Province following suit with another secession, which would mean the loss of more than one-third of the wealthiest lands in the Republic of the Congo. Russell believed his job was secure, but he wasn't as confident about his personal safety. Spontaneous violence erupted with frequency, spreading fast with the fury of a brush fire. As a result, thousands of citizens had died over the past year. Nobody was safe, and the pace of the country's disintegration bewildered him. In the struggle for control of the Republic, the Congo became the pawn of the Belgian Army, the United States, the Soviet Union, and the military forces of the United Nations. Russell feared being purged because he was in favor of the Katanga secession. He desperately wanted to leave the Congo, but Stella didn't want to because she wanted to see Mwezi and Esy again. She hoped they would live at her house.

"If I were Hackett Salomon, I would be afraid for my life," Russell said. "He started the secessionist movement, and there are angry protesters that would like his neck."

"Does he have a body guard? My job would disappear if anything would happen to him."

"Don't forget that you and Mwezi have a place to live. We want you back home."

"Everything is so uncertain, but this job has provided us good food and a safe place to stay. I don't know if I want to go back to your house."

"Please, please come back, Esy," Russell said. "I worry about Stella. She misses you and Mwezi so much. She's so unhappy."

"I don't know what to do. I'm sorry that Stella is miserable, but Mwezi and I have a good life here. I'm able to save money for his future, and we are taken care of very well here."

"What can I tell Stella?"

"Tell her we are fine and that I don't know what to do."

"Can I come to talk to you in a week?"

"Yes, do you want the same time?"

"Yes," Russell said. "Thank you, Esy."

It was hard to process the visits from Russell. Everything got so complicated with the Cox family. She had cooked and cleaned the house for them, and tried to make them happy by giving them a baby to nurture and enjoy. But no matter how much she gave them, it was not enough. Stella had been extremely angry with her the last time they talked. Esy was hurt and Mwezi felt the rejection as well. When Stella stopped caring for Mwezi, it left her no recourse but to take Mwezi and run away. Stella broke her promise. Entertaining the thought of reconciling with Stella was painful. She wondered if she could ever trust Stella again.

☙☙☙

"Hackett is coming here this morning to check on things. We've got to make everything clean and organized. He hates disorder and clutter," Hilda said, as she walked briskly into Esy and M's room. Esy sat up straight in her bed, but M, sensing the change in mood, wanted to make everyone laugh. He stood up, jumped up and down on the bed and threw his pillow at Hilda hoping to start a pillow fight.

"Oh, M," Hilda groaned. "You can't be a little monkey today. I'll give him some breakfast, and take him to the park so you can clean your room and get ready."

"Thanks, Hilda."

Esy bathed, picked up the room, and took the dirty

laundry to the other side of the house. She was grateful M was potty-trained, and that she had taken the time to fold the washed clothes and put them in drawers. The room upstairs needed to be cleaned. It had been a late night the night before, and she was exhausted. With a bucket of soapy water in hand and clean sheets in the other, she climbed the steps.

"Hackett here." Esy heard his brusque shout from the bottom of the stairs. "Where's Hilda?"

Esy placed the sheets on the bed and set the pail down before going downstairs to greet Hackett.

"Hilda took Mwezi to the park, so I could clean the rooms," she responded.

"Mwezi is taking too much time away from the work she needs to do," he snapped. "You'll have to take care of your own son from now on. Where's Asha?"

"I don't know," Esy said. "She might be still in her room."

"Tell her to get up. I need to talk to both of you."

"Asha, Hackett's here," she said. "He needs to talk to us. You've got to get up."

"Why is he here?" Asha asked.

"I'm not sure. He says he needs to talk to both of us."

"All right," Asha grumbled.

Asha hastily put on her clothes and met Hackett and Esy in the kitchen. With a foot on the chair and elbow on his knee, Hackett talked with the full-throated voice of authority.

"Esy is bringing more money than you are, Asha," he said. "Something has to change. I have another girl who is interested in working the room, so you've got to do a better job."

"I'll try," Asha said shocked at the unexpected rebuke.

"I have a friend who is a colonel in the Belgian army. He must have the best. Esy, you would be right for him. He wants you to come into the room on your knees." Hackett said.

"Did he say why he wants that?" Esy asked.

"He wants to be the master and you, a slave. He'll tip you very well if you obey. When can you see him?"

Esy was uncomfortable but stayed quiet.

"Did you hear me?"

"Yes."

"Then, answer me!"

"I have time tomorrow night."

"I'll let him know."

Hackett took his foot off the kitchen chair, turned his back toward them, and stomped out of the house, slamming the door behind him. Hilda had returned during his rant, but had slipped into her bedroom with M to avoid a confrontation.

"Hackett doesn't stop by often, but when he does it's never good," Hilda said. "Did I miss anything when I was out?"

"He threatened my job and he's having Esy service a friend of his," Asha said. "I don't know which one is worse."

"Mommy," M said as he toddled over to hug her.

Having sensed a dark mood in the house, M clung to his mother the rest of the day. His usual happy disposition changed to fear and apprehension. The events of the day haunted Esy too. Hackett threatened Asha, threatened her son's well being, and thrust his friend on her. It all seemed so peculiar. Esy wondered if the uprisings and the secession of Katanga Province might have something to do with Hackett's agitation.

ↁↁↁ

Esy compulsively cleaned and organized the room in preparation for the colonel. She even changed the sheets a second time because the first set didn't smell right. With her prettiest outfit and hair just so, she was as ready as she would ever be.

Hilda brought the colonel to the room while Esy waited for him in the bathroom. After opening the door, she approached him on her knees, purposely not making eye contact. Her eyes quickly caught sight of a blonde man with a face of steel, who stood tall and erect. His austere brown uniform with red beret announced a threatening presence. His lips hardly moved as he yelled for her to come to him by the bed. His voice was like a machine talking.

"Come here, little slave girl!" he shouted as he moved toward her. He took a knife out of its sheath and she heard the snap of a switchblade and saw a metallic flash as he brandished the weapon. Horrified, Esy's heart pounded against her chest wall. She was like a rabbit in the wild, petrified with fear when pounced by a predator. She tried hard to hang to her consciousness, but to no avail, fear took possession of her senses and she passed out. In a dreamlike state she felt her body transition from no pain to excruciating pain.

Searing pain deep in her pelvis woke Esy out of her swoon. She looked down at herself and panicked. Blood pooled between her legs, then dripped down the side of the bed. She looked around for the colonel, afraid to move, but she was alone—he had gone. She tried to swing her legs out of the bed to stand, but the intense pain doubled her over, and she fell on the floor. *What did he do to me? Did he stab me? Did he stick a knife in my womb? I feel weak. I must get help.*

"Hilda," she screamed.

At Esy's frantic cry, Hilda ran up the stairs leaving M behind in the kitchen. She found Esy lying on the floor in a pool of blood. Hilda lifted her and struggled with her down the stairs to a couch and then, called an ambulance. After a quick inspection of Esy's injuries, Hilda clasped her hands over her mouth as she wailed. With shaking hands, Hilda placed a blanket over Esy to keep her warm and then, sat next to her, took Esy's hand in hers, and waited for the ambulance.

"Dear Lord, please keep this beautiful young Mother alive. Make her well and whole again," Hilda pleaded.

CHAPTER 7

Turning Back...

ങ്ങങ്ങങ്ങ

Asha heard the ambulance arrive and raced downstairs to find Esy on the couch, the pallor of death on her face. "What happened?"

"I'm not sure. I think the colonel must have attacked her. She's bleeding heavily from the lacerations. She's barely conscious," Hilda said, as she sat stroking Esy's hand.

Hilda ushered the ambulance driver and medic to Esy's side. Without hesitating a moment, they hoisted her gently onto a gurney and wheeled her out of the house.

"I'll go to the hospital with her," Hilda said, as the men loaded Esy into the ambulance, her voice soft but urgent.

"No, I'm sorry Ma'am, there is no room in the ambulance."

"Is there room in the front seat?"

"Well, I suppose we can squeeze you in the middle."

"Thank you. Thank you," Hilda said. She turned to Asha. "I left M in the kitchen. Please watch him for me."

"Oh, poor M! Of course I'll care for him," Asha said.

Asha didn't stay to watch the ambulance pull away, instead went to the kitchen to find M. He was sitting at the table, eyes wide, face streaked with teardrops. Tears streamed down Asha's face too as she took him in her arms and rocked him.

"Where's Mommy?" Mwezi said.

"Mommy needs a doctor because she is hurt. She had to go to the hospital to get it fixed. The doctors at the hospital will take good care of her and I'll take you to see her as soon as I can."

The rocking soothed Mwezi, who sighed and hiccupped between each sob. This was M's second wound caused by evil hearts and minds—the first was Stella's rejection, which made him cry--creating insecurity. One day he was the "apple of her" eye and the next day, her jealous rage banished him to the basement and she wouldn't even look at him. Esy took especially good care of him during that time—lavished him with attention, made sure he had food and tucked him in at night. She sang him to sleep with lullabies. And now, a cruel and demonic misogynist injured his sweet mother, the innocent victim of a heart so cruel and depraved that her very life hung in the balance. This sharp turn of events created an uncertain future for both the child and mother. Her only "crime" was to provide for the needs of her son, to love him the best she could.

Asha was sad and scared too. She knew that violence was a real possibility for any girl doing the kind of work she and Esy were doing. Up until this horrific attack, Hilda had taken good care of them. How could anyone prepare for something like this? Why did this happen?

ᘓᘓᘓ

The Katanga Province seceded from the First Republic and Hackett Salomon orchestrated the secession. The Belgian army and the United Nations Military forces were dead set against his action. Hackett had enemies … many enemies. These military forces had first hand knowledge of how integral the Katanga mines were to the financial well being of the Congo as a whole. The cobalt, the nickel and the copper kept the economic wheels turning. Hackett didn't care about the turmoil or how many of Katanga's people were endangered. Concerned only with his selfish interest, he just wanted to keep his industrial monopoly. The country's prosperity was the least of his concerns, and it was likely that Esy was one of the spoils of this violent rebellion, a brutal counterattack against Hackett's political agenda.

ᘓᘓᘓ

All the rocking made M fall sleep at last. Asha laid him in bed with care and closed the door and went to her own bedroom to try to get some sleep.

She awoke the next the morning to sun shining through her bedroom window. She got up quickly, first going to find Hilda to ask about Esy. But Hilda wasn't there. Perhaps she hadn't returned from the hospital. Using the house phone, Asha dialed the hospital and asked for Hilda, who was a friend of Esy, their patient.

"Hello." Hilda's voice was low and raspy from exhaustion.

"Hi, Hilda. This is Asha. I'm calling to see how Esy is doing."

"She's not well. They had to give her blood transfusions because she lost so much blood, and they had to wait for a surgeon. She's been in emergency surgery since three this morning. From the conference I had with the Doctor, he indicated she suffered severe damage to her bladder. He hopes the surgery will remove the threat of a potential fistula and incontinence."

"What is a fistula?"

"I'm not completely sure, but the Doctor said the severe stab wounds affected the channels of elimination. Hackett came and talked to him last night. He's furious and disgusted with the colonel, but not for Esy's sake. I heard him yelling, 'that bastard destroyed my money train!'"

"Both Hackett and the colonel are despicable men! Poor Esy. She didn't deserve to be treated like this."

"How is M?" Hilda asked.

"He's asleep right now, but he woke up crying earlier in the night, and he started that nasty cough again. I'm worried about him."

"Do you have anyone scheduled for tonight?"

"Just one at eleven."

"I'll be home as soon as I can."

∽∽∽∽∽

M woke up in the night with a worrisome cough. Asha felt his forehead and detected a high fever. The poor child coughed so much he vomited. She gave him water and milk and walked him up and down the hallway. She wished so much that Esy were here to take care of him. Asha had never taken care of a sick baby before. She had minded her little brother, but only to keep him out of trouble.

Asha listened for Hilda's return, relieved when she heard the front door open.

"Hilda, I'm so glad you're home," she cried, still holding the lethargic baby.

"I have good news," Hilda said. "Esy will be okay. It was a vicious attack, but she will survive. She suffered deep wounds to her bladder. They don't know for sure, but she might be incontinent for the rest of her life. It will be about six months or more before she heals completely." Then, she frowned noticing the child in her arms. "What's happened here? How is he?"

"Besides missing his mommy, he has a fever and that nasty cough is back," Asha said.

"Let me hold him." Hilda lifted Mwezi into her arms and rocked him.

No sooner did Mwezi nod off to sleep, than the coughing would start and wake him up. Hilda tried to comfort him, but nothing worked. During his next coughing spasm, Hilda saw blood in the phlegm, which startled her. "Oh! My! We need to take him to the hospital right away."

Asha found his clothes, dressed him, and packed some toys.

"Hilda, you get some sleep. I'll take M to the hospital." Asha counted the money in her purse, and then wrapped the baby in a blanket.

"After I've had a few hours of sleep, I'll come to the hospital and relieve you," Hilda said, yawning.

Asha left for the emergency room. This was her first time taking a child to a hospital. Medical treatment was something her family couldn't afford. Once she got over the strong antiseptic smell, she found the hospital in Elisabethville surprisingly clean and orderly, much better than the one in her village. The Europeans were the only ones in the Congo who could afford good medical care. Poor people in the rural areas of the country had few medical resources, and most of the clinics didn't even have electricity. That meant no refrigeration for medications. The so-called clinic in her village had no roof, which made it impossible to keep any medical equipment.

This hospital in Elisabethville was much better than any in the villages, but there was still a long wait. It took the nurses and doctors five hours before they could see M.

After the Doctor examined M, he sighed and sat in a chair. "This young man has a severe case of pneumonia," he said. "We have to work on getting that fever down. He's going to need plenty of rest and liquids to get him out of this. I have medicine that will help with the infection. It is expensive." Asha's eyes opened wide at the figure he named. "Can you afford it?"

"Yes, I'll pay for the medication."

The doctor left the room and returned with a bottle of liquid and told her to follow the directions on the bottle. Asha dug into her purse to pay for the medicine knowing this was a kind favor for her dear friend. Asha couldn't read, so she needed Hilda to read the directions on the bottle.

"Bring him back in if he coughs up blood again or if you don't see any improvement."

"I will," she promised.

Asha's steps were slow as she headed back to the house. Her exhaustion was catching up with her. When they returned, she tried to get M to take a little food, but he was too sick to be hungry. As she was rocking him to sleep, Hilda opened the bedroom door.

"How's M?"

"He has pneumonia. I need you to read the directions on the medicine." Asha said as Hilda read the directions out loud.

"I'm not surprised it's pneumonia," Hilda said. "Those months of exposing his lungs to the cobalt dust in the mine must have weakened them."

"I fed him, but he wasn't interested in food."

"Good for you. You'll make a good mother one day," Hilda said.

M's head became heavy on Asha's arm and he drifted into a sound sleep. After she was certain of he wouldn't wake up, she placed him in his bed with tenderness, pulled the curtains across the windows, and tiptoed out of the bedroom. Asha found Hilda slumped over at the kitchen table with her hands over her face.

"I'm ready to get out of this business," Hilda said. "Esy's injuries are the worse I've seen. He could have killed her."

"I talked with one of my patrons and he shared that men get even with each other by mistreating and raping their women," Asha asked. "Do you think that's true?"

"Yes it is very true, especially in the Congo," Hilda said. "Women are the spoils of war and they're ravaged and raped by men all the time. The colonel was from Belgium and he was angry that the Katanga Province claimed independence. Most likely, he was getting even with Hackett."

"Why didn't Hackett know that?"

"From what I understand, the colonel was a classmate of his when he was studying in Belgium. He assumed the relationship he had with the colonel would overrule any anger he had about the political movement. He was *dead* wrong. I just hope that Esy will survive this."

"Me, too," Asha said. "I'm thinking about a change myself. But what made you decide to work here in the first place?"

"My husband knew Hackett. The mob killed my husband Dante during the uprising after Patrice Lumumba's murder. I didn't have any place to go. Hackett offered me this job." Hilda shrugged. "I needed a roof over my head and food to eat. Until now, it has been a good job."

"Where are your children?"

"They all moved to Leopoldville to find work. My oldest son barely escaped with his life during the rebellion following the murder. I don't hear from them often, but as far as I know, they all survived."

"Did you come here alone from Belgium?"

"No, my sister Frieda Van Tyl and I came to the Belgian Congo because of her job. She works for an international school in Elisabethville. I met my husband through Frieda's school when I first came to the Congo. He is…was a teacher there. His death opened my eyes to my situation, an unemployed stranger in a strange land. When he died, my life seemed to be over. I miss him so much."

"Hilda, that's an amazing story. My story is so different."

"Were you born in Elisabethville?"

"No, I was born near the little village of Kipushi. My daddy was killed in a mining accident so my mother had to go to work. She is a domestic for a Canadian family. The man of the family is an engineer for the Ivanhoe mine near our home. My job was to take care of my little brother Dabuka, who was a troublemaker. I used to get so frustrated with him because he wouldn't listen to me. He's working in the Ivanhoe mine now."

"Do you see your mother and brother?"

"Maybe once a year. All of us are working hard at our jobs."

"Well, I should go to the hospital to visit Esy. Do you want to come with me?"

"Yes. I'll check to see if M is awake," Asha said.

৫৩৫৩৫৩

Esy greeted Hilda, Asha, and Mwezi with a weak hello and a smile as they entered her hospital room. She looked good considering all she had been through. Thanks to the medicine and a good sleep, M was feeling much better too, and was excited to see his mommy. Without thinking, Esy held out her arms to hug and hold him, but discovered lifting him was too painful.

"Mommy has to heal a little more before I can hold you," Esy said to her little boy. "Soon, I will be able to carry you, but for now we can hold hands." Hilda pulled up a chair and sat M on her lap so he could hold his mother's hand.

Hilda and Asha discussed M's illness with her. Esy blamed the mine for his weakened condition and herself for taking him there. Grateful that the medicine was working, she was also thankful for her loyal friends. "I don't know if that weakened lung condition can be reversed. I feel guilty about it. Thank you so very much for taking M to the Doctor," Esy said to Asha. "I'll pay you back."

"And I thank you too, Hilda. I might have died if you hadn't taken me to the hospital. I don't know what would happen to M if you didn't care for him…if he couldn't stay with you." She looked from Hilda to Asha. "You are good friends." After exchanging careful embraces, she continued. "I have a special request. When you visit me next time would you bring my mother's journal? It's under my mattress."

"I will. I promise," Asha said.

Fate had dealt each of them cruel blows. Hilda had lost her husband, Asha had lost her father, Esy had lost her mother and almost died from an assault. Fate had forced them to make hard choices, but they were all strong and they prevailed. Friendship united the three of them into a unit of healing. They needed each other. They felt thankful for being alive and most of all, that Esy was recovering from what could have been a fatal assault. Being together was to be celebrated.

God answers prayers, Esy thought.

The nurse entered Esy's room to take her vitals and Hilda asked, "Do you know when Esy will be able to go home?"

"It will be a while. The doctor wants the bleeding to stop before he discharges her. The stab wounds went very deep," the nurse said, as she made notes in the chart at the end of her bed before leaving to complete her rounds.

"Have the police been here to ask questions?" Asha asked.

"No."

"Because the assault took place in a brothel, I don't think the police will take this crime seriously," Hilda replied.

"What do you mean?" Esy asked.

"Well, you know, they think because of what you do you deserve any trouble that comes your way." Asha, Hilda, and M went back to the house to have dinner leaving Esy alone with her thoughts.

CRCRCR

Esy understood the harsh reality that working for Hackett had meant—she was not protected by the law. It unsettled her to know Hackett looked out only for himself and for ways to make more money at her expense. She was sick and tired of being a servant and being exploited. What Hilda said haunted her …"I don't think the police will take this assault seriously." *Am I a dog that can be kicked around? If someone murders me do the police look the other way? Do they say—she's just a prostitute, she's not important? But, I am important to M. He would be without a mommy. Wouldn't the colonel have to take responsibility for that? Shouldn't he be punished?*

Esy waited, drifting in and out of sleep, for the Doctor to come and give her more information about her condition, and about what was next. The early evening shadows dimmed the room long before he came to her room during his final rounds for the day.

"Hello, Esy," he said, as he looked at his chart. "I have some good news and some bad news."

Esy pulled herself up despite the pain as she braced herself for the report.

"During surgery, we were able to open the channels of evacuation, which means the surgery was a success. It prevented a potential fistula. This is important because sepsis is always a concern if that isn't corrected. However, your bladder was damaged to such an extent that it's likely that you will be incontinent for the rest of your life. Significant scar tissue may also develop and require further treatment."

Esy thought about this for a moment. Incontinent. "Does this mean that I have to wear diapers all the time for the rest of my life?"

"It's a possibility," he hedged with a touch of sympathy. "We don't know for sure."

"When will I be able to go home?"

"In a couple of days," he said. "I want to make sure the bleeding is under control."

"That seems like a long way off. That's a long time to be without my baby boy. Good night, Doctor," Esy said as she turned her head to the wall.

"Good night," he said.

Esy heard the door swish closed behind him.

Alone with her thoughts, Esy struggled to think of a way through this tough situation. She had a mountain of grief to sort out. Her feelings were complicated. She was relieved that her life had been spared, but she would have to suffer the humiliation of chronic bladder problems. For sure, she would have to change occupations, but where would she go? Who would give her employment? Perhaps she would have to be a servant again, somewhere else. Underneath, something was simmering and gnawing at her. She knew she would have to make a change—it was inevitable. Making these hard decisions was too much sometimes. If she were to go back to live with Stella and Russell, her relationship with Stella would have to mend. Esy had M to consider and she uttered a weary sigh. In reality, her choices were pain… or more pain. Her thoughts weighed on her until she trailed off into a restless sleep.

CRCRCR

"Here's your mother's diary," Asha said when she came to visit the next day. "I found it where you said it would be."

"Oh thank you," Esy placed it on her chest and held it tight. "Did you leave M with Hilda?"

"Yes. He started that horrible cough again, so Hilda is home taking care of him. We didn't want to take him out."

"I'm so worried about him. I think he has something seriously wrong with him."

"He'll get better when his mommy can take care of him. Did the doctor tell you when you could come home?"

"He told me I could leave once the bleeding is under control—maybe in a couple of days."

"Have you heard from Hackett?" Asha asked.

"No."

"He should pay for your medical expenses," Asha explained. "After all, it was his "friend" who stabbed you. He's the one who put you in a dangerous situation."

"The medical bills could use up all my savings." Esy's frowned. "I've set that money aside for Mwezi's education."

"This is Hilda's day off, so I'll head home to take care of M so she can enjoy some time off. Good-bye, Esy." She couldn't find any words of comfort.

"Good-bye, friend."

Esy opened her mother's journal and read:

My Dear Child,

I have had so much sorrow in my life. Your daddy and I struggled hard from time to time. I didn't like to fight so I just got quiet. He talked bad to me when he was angry, but I tried not to get angry. He dominated me and I usually gave in. I hope you find a husband that will love you without having to be a boss.

Over the years, I have had to learn how to forgive and I tried very hard to keep my faith strong. Esy, always

remember to "…pray for those that despitefully use you and persecute you." Mathew 5:44.
Love,
Mama

"Pray for those that despitefully use you?" *Did you really mean that, Mama? That beast has ruined my life and I'm supposed to pray for him? That doesn't make any sense to me. I get so angry when I think about how hard I tried to make the room nice for him. I changed the sheets twice to make sure they smelled fresh. Lavender scent filled the room—I did that so the room would be relaxing. I was so violated, and to think that I spent all that effort only to be brutalized by him. Well, Mama, I love you and you have been wise much of the time, but in this instance, what you're saying is pure nonsense!* Esy slammed the cover of the diary shut and slapped it down on the table next to her. Disgusted, she was staring at the wall by her bed in a trance when she heard a man's voice.

"Good evening," Hackett said.

What's he doing here? She thought, and turned her head toward him, looking straight into his eyes. "I am angry. This shouldn't have happened to me."

"How do you think *I* feel? I gave you and your…" he hesitated, "son a place to live. I fed you, bought your clothes, gave you grooming lessons. Now, I see a broken woman. You're useless to me."

"I've worked hard for you in the mine and in that house. I need you to pay my medical bills. The money I've saved is for Mwezi's future. I don't want to spend his money on my medical bills."

"I'm *not* paying your medical expenses!"

Mama, how can you tell me to forgive this hateful man?

"I'm not paying *your* medical bills!" Hackett shouted.

"What is going on?" Esy's nurse demanded, barging into the room and interrupting Hackett's tirade.

"*Nothing* is going on," he yelled, as he stormed out of the room slamming the door with a violence that belied the words he said.

Esy was livid.

"Now, now, you mustn't get upset. You'll hurt yourself and take longer to heal." Her nurse tried to comfort and calm her.

Esy's anger dissolved into tears. Overcome with worry and hopelessness, she cried until she collapsed with exhaustion. Sadness like a chilly fog surrounded her as she succumbed to a deep sleep.

ღღღ

The fog lifted by the time Esy woke up. Her rage and tears were a catharsis, a cleansing. She felt free because it purged and delivered her from evil. Praying had helped Esy in the past, and now, asking God to help her heal felt right to her.

"Dear God in heaven, renew my energy, and heal my wounds so I can be a good Mother to Mwezi. You have given me a son, a wonderful gift. I will always be grateful. Amen." A spirit of determination rose within her. Although evil, sadistic men had tried to crush her, they only made her become more resolved to raise a kind, caring young man, one who respected and valued women. With her single-mindedness, she could make that happen.

CRCRCR

Esy was the first patient the doctor saw the next morning. He came shortly after her nurse checked her vitals. There was a bounce in his step. He read the notes on the clipboard at the foot of the bed.

"Well, it looks like you're ready to go home later today. Your bleeding is under control. There can be no lifting, running or sweeping. You *must* rest!" he admonished. "There's full-blown rioting on the streets, but the riots don't last all day. Late afternoon usually brings quiet. We'll release you after the dust settles to keep you safe." He looked up from her chart. "Your appetite seems to be back, but we'll know more after lunch and dinner. You are doing well."

"I'm ready to go home, but I have some questions for my after care. Will I have to wear a diaper all the time?"

"It's possible that your bladder will heal, but the damage to the sphincter muscle and the urethra was so severe that it's unlikely that you'll regain your former control."

"I hoped you wouldn't say that," Esy said, dejection showing in her sagging shoulders and somber eyes.

"You are a young lady, and it is unfortunate this has happened, but it could have been worse. I treated someone with a severe fistula last week, and she died from sepsis."

"Will I be able to have more children?"

"I don't know, but you probably will have a different sensation when you have intercourse. You might experience a great deal of pain."

"Well, that's not good news," Esy said.

"If you have more questions, please come and see me."

"Thank you for all you've done, Doctor."

The Doctor left the room, quietly shutting the door behind him.

I wonder what my future will be like? Will I find love and have a family? Will M have a brother or sister? What can I do to give M a better life? Esy's emotions vacillated. One moment she teemed with confidence and the next moment she felt destroyed. How could she make sense of this cruel predicament?

Esy ate a good lunch and dinner. She packed her clothes and her mother's diary, then, she made her way down the hall to find Hilda waiting with M. Her purpose became clear as she reached for her son.

"I've missed you so much," she said, kneeling to embrace M as a single tear of joy rolled down her cheek. Holding his warm little body against her firmed her resolve. They had an unbreakable bond and would brave the world together. The threesome walked home hand in hand with M in the middle keeping up with the adults on both sides.

"Esy, I wanted to let you know that Russell is waiting for you at the house," Hilda said. "He wants to talk with you."

"I wonder what he has to say."

Passing a newsstand, Esy read the headlines in the newspaper, *Mjumbe* which stated that the Katanga province had successfully seceded from the Republic of the Congo and that Moise Tshombe was now the President of the State of Katanga and Elisabethville, the capital. She read on and at the bottom of the page another headline in smaller print caught her eye:

"Hackett Salomon Murdered During Riots"

"Hilda, What does this mean?"

"I know one thing for sure that Hackett was front and center. He was asking for trouble. He led the charge. This was something he had wanted for a long time. The United Nations and the Republic of Congo are unhappy, because the mining is crucial for the economy of the country. I don't want to share too much about how I feel in public. These are dangerous times, so let's not talk about it now. We can talk about it when we get home."

CRCRCR

So eager to get home, Esy wanted to scoop M up in her arms, but was unable to carry him, so they continued the walk home at M's pace. She laughed with glee as she opened the front door, but came to an abrupt halt when she saw Russell Cox in the kitchen. She had mixed emotions about Mwezi meeting his father after leaving the Cox home with a cloud over their heads. Fortunately, Mwezi was too young to remember that time. It was important to her that the meeting with his father be a blessing, not a curse. She wanted only the best for her cherished son.

"Hello, Esy," a somber Russell greeted her. "How are you feeling?"

"I've been in the hospital for over a week, and I'm feeling stronger each day." Esy said, as she released M's hand. He hid behind her while he peered around her skirt to scrutinize Russell.

"Hi, Mwezi. Oh my, you have grown! You're walking already." Russell looked at Esy for permission to hold him. She gave him a quick nod, and he lifted him up into his arms and gave him a kiss on the cheek. "You are a fine young lad." M sensed something important about the hug and the kiss. He pulled his head back and stared at Russell's face and then, gave him a big smile.

How can I keep those two apart? They have a special connection. I think M will like his daddy.

"Esy, I want to talk to you in private," Russell said. Hilda exchanged a look with Esy before she walked M to his room. Esy sat and Russell straddled the chair across the table from her. "Have you given any thought about coming back to live with Stella and me?"

"Yes, I've thought about it often, especially when I was recuperating in the hospital. I have some questions."

"Ask me anything."

"First of all, Hackett refused to pay for my medical treatment. I am hoping you will help me pay that bill, so I can keep my savings secure for my son's education."

"I'll pay for the whole bill," Russell said.

"Thank you so much!" Esy responded. "Also, I want to finish high school, so I can get a good job. Would you or Stella be willing to take care of M when I go to classes?"

"I've talked to Stella about that and she said she would be overjoyed to take care of him."

"What if Stella gets jealous again, and is mean to me or M? What will happen to us?"

"I've thought about that too. I'll pay for an apartment for you and Mwezi if that happens."

"Why should I trust you? How do I know you'll remember if the time comes when we must move?" Esy's brown dyes drilled him until he looked away.

I'll put it in writing and give it to you to keep," Russell said.

"Also, I want you to claim Mwezi as your son so he can become a Belgian citizen."

"Why do you want that?"

"David from the mission station advised me. He strongly recommended that you take responsibility for your son. If you had helped me support him, I wouldn't have worked for Hackett and met that evil man that injured me." Esy turned away to think of her next words. "I want him to take your name and have his citizenship documented. If he is a Belgian citizen, he can go to school there without waiting for the bureaucracy to process the endless paperwork, and much of his schooling will be paid by the state. I want the best education for Mwezi. He is very bright."

"Yes, Mwezi is a fine lad, and he is the only son I know I have. I can agree to all those conditions. When can you move back to the house?"

"Not so fast. I want to read the papers before you and I sign them, and also, I want to talk to Stella before I agree to come back."

"I'll have the papers ready by the end of the week. I'm sure Stella will talk to you anytime. She is lonely and misses Mwezi. This separation has been hard on her."

"I have been worried that Hackett would take all my savings to pay for the medical bills, but I don't have to worry about that any more. Hackett was murdered during the riots last night."

"Really? Are you sure that it's not just a rumor? I'm not surprised because he's made so many enemies. There has been so much killing and fighting that the confusion makes it hard to know who's alive or dead," Russell said.

"I saw the headline on the bottom of the front page of the newspaper.

"In some ways, he was a strong leader, but he sure was a mean man."

"It's going to be some time before I can forgive him," Esy said.

ଔଔଔ

"Come in." Stella shouted.

Esy opened the door to find Stella slouched in the living room chair, her back to the front door, and dressed in a bathrobe and slippers. She looked glum. "Esy, it has been a long time since I've seen you."

"How are you doing?"

"Not so good. I miss taking care of Mwezi. He brought me so much joy."

"I've talked with Russell and he said that you want M and me to move back in. Is that true?"

"Who's M?"

"That's Mwezi's nickname."

"Okay. Yes, I want to have the both of you back in the house. I miss you."

"I worry about you rejecting M and me again."

"I'm sorry I did that to you. I wish it never happened. My heart was broken and I let my emotions run amok. It makes me sad not having you around. I know that now. You and Mwezi bring me such joy."

"I need to finish high school so I can find a good job. I need you to take care of M while I'm at school. I have to be able to depend on that."

"I promise from the bottom of my heart that you can depend on me. Will you forgive me for going on a rampage the last time you were here?"

"Yes, I forgive you, Stella."

Stella and Esy hugged, driven together by the intensity of the moment. A genuine connection was made, heart to heart. They needed each other for life giving support, for a kind of emotional sustenance. "When do you want M and me to move in?"

"As soon as possible! Oh Esy, I'm so happy." Stella said, as tears welled up in her eyes. "Let me show you your room. I have a surprise."

Patch was stretched out on her bed. He nuzzled and purred as Esy stroked his soft shiny fur. Stella pointed out all the changes she had made in the room. There was a partition in the middle of the room dividing the space into two bedrooms. It was smaller than before, of course, but the new feature was that M's bedroom was next to hers. The rooms were together and private at the same time. When Esy peeked into M's bedroom, she smiled at the boyishness of it all. Plastering the walls were pictures of sports cars with a picture of Russell's little Austin-Healy Sprite having a prominent place in the décor. It was a delightful space for her son.

"Do you like it?" Stella asked

"Yes, very much. M likes bright colors, so he'll be happy," Esy said, smiling.

Esy was satisfied with the change in the relationship between her and Stella. She seemed to understand what she had done to her was cruel and resulted in her life being disrupted almost beyond repair. There was always a chance something might happen again, but she had Russell's backing. It gave her confidence. *Russell said he would never touch me that way again, and I hope he keeps his promise. Stella is penitent and sorry for what she did, but I need to be on guard with her. If all goes well, this is much better than the painful suffering I had when I worked for Hackett. I want to finish high school, so I can create a better life for M.*

ᘉᘉᘉ

Hilda and Asha had supported and cared for her and Mwezi during the tragic event. Esy was deeply indebted to them. Not having them around would be a hard adjustment for her.

"Hilda, I want to do something for you to say thank you for all you've done," Esy said.

"Take care of yourself and bring M around once in awhile. He brings me joy and makes me laugh."

"I will do that. Thank you. When I'm done with my education and become a famous businesswoman, I'll hire you and you can get away from this kind of work," Esy said with a chuckle.

"I had something very good happen in my life. My father died a year ago and left money in a trust for Frieda and me. It's not a whole lot, but I should have enough."

"That's wonderful—not that your father died, but that he left something for you."

Next stop was Asha's room. Knocking on the door reminded Esy of the time she found Asha sobbing in her bedroom because Hackett had sent her to another mine. *With Asha being at another mine, I was easy prey. I look back at his actions and see how devious he was. He was a predator of the worst kind. I feel such relief that he's no longer on this earth.*

"Good morning, Asha," Esy noticed how frazzled and exhausted she looked. It must have been a difficult night.

"Hi, friend. You look so much better than you did a

week ago. So glad you're feeling better. It was so unfair that you had to suffer like that. I worry every night I work that someone will brutalize me."

"Is everything going okay with your patrons?"

"Yes, it's going okay, but I want a change."

"Who is going to be the boss now that Hackett is dead?"

"I think his name is Viktor or something. I can't remember."

Esy grimaced, but she knew that this was not the time to express worry.

"I'll say a prayer for you each day hoping you'll stay safe. It's a dangerous business you're in. I wanted you to know that M and I are moving out."

"What? When did this happen?" Asha said, in shock.

"Russell was here when I came home from the hospital and he begged me to come back and live with them. I decided to give it a try. He did say that if it doesn't work out, he'll pay for an apartment for M and me."

"Do you think you'll get back to school?"

"I hope so, and I want to get Mwezi into a good school."

"You are such a good Mama and a good friend. I'm going to miss you a lot."

"You'll have to come a visit M and me. If I find a better job for you, I'll let you know." Esy said, as she hugged her friend good-bye.

છ છ છ

Looking forward to the next chapters of their lives, M and Esy started down the road to the Cox residence.

M was happy that he had a room next to his mommy. He tolerated all the hugs and kisses Stella gave him, but most of all, he liked the rides Russell gave him in his little red car.

This was a time of relative calm in their lives. There was order in the Cox home, Esy prepared the evening meal and Stella did the laundry and kept the house clean. This order was a welcomed change and meant that Esy had a better, more consistent schedule with evenings free. They had good meals on the table and comfortable accommodations. Most of all, M had a Daddy and they were enjoying each other.

True to her word, Esy visited Hilda and Asha at least once a month. Motivated by greater profits, Viktor von Peters had added more girls to the brothel. This was a risky business practice because brothels were illegal. Hilda was paid handsomely for her efforts, and when Asha was given the opportunity to move to Kinshasa, where prostitution was legal and she could make more money, she leapt at it.

Esy was sad to see her friend leave Elisabethville, but she visited Hilda often with M as promised. M and Hilda had an amusing relationship filled with teasing and practical jokes. One such visit was particularly memorable. Hilda had switched the salt and sugar, putting sugar in the saltshaker. M lavishly put "salt" on his popcorn. The look he gave after the first bite was unforgettable. His eyes popped open wide, followed by a piercing look at Hilda, which was followed by a contagious laugh.

Another time, M tucked a plastic spider in his pocket and placed it on his head when Hilda wasn't looking. When Hilda saw it, laughter filled the air.

Over the years, Hilda watched M grow from a toddler to a youngster, to a teen-ager, and to a young man.

Esy went back to school and excelled in her studies. For her, the stars of the universe were aligned. She enjoyed watching her funny son grow into a young man, and she looked forward to time spent with Hilda. It was quite another story, however, for her beloved country, which at that time was called the First Republic of the Congo.

CHAPTER 8

Mwezi's World

ભ્ય ભ્ય ભ્ય

My son, Mwezi has been the driving force behind my life and my reason for living. I want him to be educated, happy and kind to women.

M grew up exposed to two cultures: one leg in the African culture and the other in the European culture. By the time Mwezi was five years old, uprisings, brutal massacres, and ineffective coup d'états plagued the ill-fated First Congolese Republic. In 1965 Lieutenant General Joseph Mobutu seized power through his control of the military. He led a successful coup and controlled the Congo with an iron fist for thirty-two years.

The chaos outside his little yellow house in Elisabethville had little effect on M, though. Stella gave him the best of care while his mommy went to school. Sheltered from the politics of the country, he had no recollection of the nightmarish time his mother suffered while working for Hackett Salomon. M's hacking cough, which often worsened in the middle of the night, reminded Esy of her time in the mines. His ailment niggled at her as she went about her day. She tried to forgive herself because it was her dire circumstance that brought about the condition. She was able to live with it when she recognized the lack of control she had over her life. She was determined to find a remedy for his weak lungs and finish her education so she could have more control over her life.

When Mwezi was old enough to attend school, his parents sent him to École International, which was considered one of the best schools in Lubumbashi. It used to be called Elisabethville, but when Mobutu's government initiated the "authenticity movement." Elisabethville was changed to Lubumbashi. The city of Leopoldville was renamed Kinshasa and Stanleyville became Kisangani.

Mwezi led a privileged life. His daddy was the main engineer for the mine near the city of Lubumbashi and his mommy was finishing her secondary education. For a brief period, M and Esy were students at that same school, and they walked hand-in-hand together each morning. Esy dropped M off with his teacher and went upstairs to her classes. At the end of the school day, the two of them would meet in the hallway and walk home together. For a while, they enjoyed an idyllic life.

One day, as Esy waited for M in the hallway by his classroom, his teacher approached her.

"We had an unusual incident today," he said. "Mwezi created a major hysteria in the classroom."

"*My* son?"

"He's in the office right now."

"What did he do?"

"The government mandated that everyone take the oral

polio vaccine. Mwezi refused, saying that we were trying to poison all the children."

"Oh no! Did you explain the vaccination to him?"

"I tried to, but he was adamant. This set off a panic with the other children, so I sent him out of the class-room. I explained the vaccination to the other children, so they settled down and took the vaccine."

"Is he still in the office?"

"Yes, and he is the only one that hasn't taken the vacci-nation. You must take him to a clinic to comply with the government polio vaccination mandate."

Esy walked toward the office, silently snickering over her son's antics. *M, you make me laugh, but I think it's good to doubt authorities especially when it involves ingest-ing something foreign. In a way, my son is a protester. He thinks for himself.* She knocked on the office door.

"Hello, I'm Mwezi's mother."

"How do you do. My name is Agu Ele. I'm the new Headmaster for the elementary school."

"Nice to meet you."

"Mwezi is in the back room. I wanted to talk with you privately. Your son was disobedient today, and he created disorder in the classroom, which caused problems for his teacher."

"I'm confused because I've trained him to ques-tion authority especially if they behave in a suspicious manner." Esy said, surprised by her own assertive words. "It's unusual for all the children to take medicine at the same time. I don't think there was sufficient explanation about what was happening. I'm proud that my son had doubts about such an unusual activity."

"Well, I disagree. We've been administering oral vaccine for five years, and this is the first time *a child* has questioned us."

"I'm sorry if I've offended you, but I want Mwezi to think for himself."

"You'll have to bring him to a clinic, because we don't want him here if he hasn't been vaccinated for polio. I'll get him from the back room."

Esy knew it would be a couple of days' wait at the clinic for M to get the vaccine, and that would mean he would miss some school. M emerged from the back room with his head down, shamefaced. During Esy and Mwezi's walk home, they talked.

Esy said, "I'm proud of you for not following the group. It is important to check with other adults if you're not sure what they expect you to do is right for you. What I've learned from all the hard times I've had is to follow what it says in the Bible, '…be ye therefore wise as serpents, and harmless as doves' (Matthew 10:16). You were wise my son, to talk with another adult before swallowing something without getting answers to your questions."

Mwezi smiled from ear to ear. The walk continued in silence.

ℭℜℭℜℭℜ

The major sport in the Congo, football (soccer), galvanized the Congolese people far more than politics or religion. At age ten, M became a leader in the sport. He executed plays with skill and cunning. He had a razor-sharp memory for what play to use for the best outcome and his athleticism, agility, and grasp of the playing field made him a valuable player. He anticipated the moves with a proficiency that was beyond his years. Also, M had a flair for the dramatic. His arms flapped like wings on the field and his long stride was smooth and synchronized. Esy, Russell, and Stella were amused by his antics and applauded every success.

ᘓᘓᘓᘓ

What started him down the athletic path was being a spectator at the championship game for the African Cup. It was 1968 and M was eight-years. Going to the event became a family affair. Stella, Russell, Esy and M went early to claim their seats and wait in the electrifying atmosphere before the game. To be the winner of the African Cup elevated the players and nation to a God-like level. The fierce competition between Ghana and the Congo created a spellbinding game for the spectators. The Congolese team triumphed which fortified the pride of its people. Loud celebrations were held everywhere in the Congo.

This victory motivated M to become a better player, so he worked hard. He dreamed of becoming a famous football star just like the members of the team who won the African Cup. His daddy, however, had a different plan for his son. He wanted M to be an engineer just like him. Russell piqued his interest in engineering. They built a go-kart and even assembled a hydraulic pump in the backyard to create a miniature waterfall. But most of all, M liked tinkering with Russell's little Austin-Healy Sprite. They worked on that car together and shared a love of sports cars. They were not only father and son, but also, good buddies.

School was easy for M. He did well in science and math, but after school on the football field he excelled.

His participation in the sport was all about making points and winning games. His mother was proud of his athletic ability and his easygoing personality. He was a likeable young man. The other team members were fair skinned, blue eyed with blonde hair. Brown eyes and dark hair were the exceptions so he stood out. When his classmates teased him about his dark skin, blue eyes, and shock of red hair, Mwezi just shrugged it off. His athleticism and intelligence gave him the confidence to offset his oddities.

During one of his football practices another player tripped him. M suffered a serious injury. He broke his foot and ankle in three places and the pain was excruciating. Even though his dad had some connections with the doctors in Elisabethville, he had to wait two days for medical attention. They cobbled up a makeshift splint, and waited for an appointment at the clinic. The doctor took one look at it and said that the foot and ankle were so mangled that they would have to insert a metal plate to align the bones and promote healing. Mwezi's surgery was successful, but the doctor ordered him not to play football for six months. He was so disheartened that he became depressed from the inertia.

Esy tried to cheer him up by making his favorite dish, chicken in mwambe sauce and chikwanga, but his lethargy continued. M's cry as an infant may have stymied Russell, but he knew how to cheer up the eleven-year-old boy. He bought M a used car, an Austin-Healy Sprite, which boosted his morale. He spent hours tinkering with his little car. His love for sports cars renewed his interest in engineering.

"I've been thinking about your education," Russell said to his son. "You'll be twelve soon, and we want to give you the best education possible. There are some good boarding schools in Belgium."

"What? You want me to leave here and go to Europe? I'll miss Mom, Stella and you," Mwezi said with a frown.

"You'll come home for visits, and I go to Belgium several times a year."

"What is a boarding school? Did you go to one?" Mwezi asked.

"Yes, I did and I loved it," Russell said. "You live with boys your age and the teachers are excellent. It is good preparation for life."

"Well, I don't want to leave my home. I like it here. Mom and Stella would miss me."

"I'll make a deal with you. Try it out for one year, and if you still want to come home, you can."

"Let me think about it. I'll let you know in a few days."

"Okay."

ᘉᘉᘉ

In the present climate of favoring African authenticity Russell wanted to preserve some of the European influence in his son. He knew Esy supported Mobutu's authenticity movement, so he planned to broaden Mwezi's political views by sending him to Belgium. He wanted his son away from the clutches of Africanization. Many cities of the Congo were already renamed. Names like Kinshasa, Kisangani, and Lubumbashi became part of the landscape. The change was too rapid for Russell.

Mobutu had been in power for just a short time, when his second military coup ousted President Kasavubu and his Prime Minister, Tshombe. Mobutu's agenda was to seize power and create his unique style of cronyism, which was based on personal loyalty between himself and his followers. There was only a pretense of political stability as Mobutu unsuccessfully tried to promote economic progress. Later in 1971, he renamed the Democratic Republic of the Congo, "Zaire," which was the third name change in eleven years. His intent was to emphasize the country's African cultural identity. Russell considered Mobutu's government to be a fragile regime. He predicted that a revolution was inevitable, and he wanted his son to stay out of harm's way.

ᘒᘒᘒ

"I thought about what you said and I have an answer," M said, while riding in the car with his father.

"What's the decision?"

"I'll try boarding school for a year to see how I like it."

"Good decision, son."

Russell gathered Stella and Esy together so M could announce his decision.

"You're too young!" Stella said.

"You're only twelve. You're still my little boy," Esy cried.

"I'm not too young. Next year I'll be taking the test for the Secondary level," M responded.

Russell waited for the clamor to die down and then, shared his approval of his son's decision. He informed them that he would pay for the tuition and boarding expenses.

"Esy, will you pay for his traveling expenses and spending money?" Russell asked.

"I will. I've been saving money for his education for a long time, but it still isn't enough. I appreciate your help, Russell."

"Mom, I know you have been working hard for my

future. Thank you. I'll study hard and you'll be proud of me," M said.

"I was twelve when I went to boarding school, and I look back at that decision and it was a good one. I think M made a good decision, too," Russell said.

CRCRCR

M went to Belgium to boarding school. Playing soccer was not a priority now that the injury had weakened his ankle. Complicating matters was the fact that the metal plate that had been screwed to bone after his original injury, had corroded, so it had to be surgically removed. The doctors in Belgium determined that his ankle had healed sufficiently, so they didn't need to insert another plate. M continued to play soccer recreationally and found good friends among his teammates.

Science and math were M's curriculum of choice, and he did well in his studies. By all appearances, M was on the way to becoming an engineer. Boarding school suited him, but the mine-induced cough still plagued him. The school personnel could not cure the disease, but they found that using a vaporizer at night eased his breathing. Russell flew to Belgium to spend time with him almost every month. They enjoyed those visits. During Christmas vacation, M flew to Lubumbashi to visit his mother and Stella.

One time, when Mwezi came home, he was almost caught up in the violence. The dramatic disintegration of the Zairean economy and the rise of anti-Mobutu sentiment among the disenfranchised led the way for two invasions of the former Katanga Province. The Congolese National Liberation Front's armed guards, operating out of Angola, plotted to overthrow the Mobutu regime. When Mwezi deplaned at the Lubumbashi airport, the soldiers held him at gunpoint while they searched for identification and rifled through his luggage for any pro-Mobutu credentials. M was in the wrong place at the wrong time. The CNLF shot and killed two people on his flight after M stepped off the plane. Fortunately, Russell arrived to meet him in time to intervene. He explained that Mwezi was a student coming home to see his family for Christmas. This was Mwezi's first-hand experience of the perils of the Congolese conflict.

Upon learning of the danger M had faced, Esy and Stella greeted him with open arms and thankful tears.

ଔଔଔଔ

M's Christmas visit was full of surprises. Esy told M that the local industries had been hiring her as a translator. This skill paid well and the demand for her translating business was expanding. The governors of the mines also discovered she could translate from French and English to Swahili. She was gaining renown, but she still had to supplement her income by waitressing at a local restaurant. M also learned that Esy was looking for an apartment to rent. Her days of subservience to Russell and Stella were ending. She wanted more control over her life. He also learned that Uncle Moyo was coming for dinner on Christmas Day. Mwezi had met him many years ago but he was too young to remember.

Stella and Russell spared no expense for Christmas, this special day when their family would be all together. They planned a European holiday feast. The aromas of baking ham, yams, dinner rolls and apple strudel mingled and swirled through the house tempting their appetites. Although Moyo straggled in late for dinner, Mwezi and Esy were happy to see him. Stella prepared a special plate for him.

"Oh, Moyo. I'm so happy to see you," shouted Esy. "Do you remember my son, Mwezi?"

"Hi, Uncle Moyo," M said as he hugged his uncle. Mwezi had grown while at school and Moyo was haggard and wasted from all the years of working in the mine. Despite the fact that Mwezi was still just a boy, the two were the same size.

"It has been a long time since I've seen you," Moyo responded, as he ate his food. "This is good," he said to Stella. "It is so different from the food I eat."

"Have you seen Dad?" Esy asked.

"I see him when he wants money. They keep him pretty busy at the mine."

"How have *you* been? Are you doing okay?" Esy asked.

"I can't work in the mine everyday. I feel weak much of the time. I cough at night and I can't sleep."

"That's not good. Have you been to see a doctor?" Esy asked.

"No, I can't afford a doctor."

"Your health matters to me. I'll bring you to my favorite clinic and get you on the list to see a doctor. The wait will probably be two or three days." Esy said.

"I can't pay for it," Moyo said, as he looked at Esy with sad eyes.

"I'll pay the bill for you." Esy said.

"That would be nice of you."

"Stella, could Moyo spend a few nights here?"

"Of course," Stella said.

After a two-day wait, Moyo saw a doctor who diagnosed him with Hard Metal Lung Disease, also known as Cobalt Lung, which had no cure, but medication could manage the symptoms. The doctor dispensed a bottle of steroid medication with instructions to follow on the bottle. Moyo thanked him for his help, and Esy paid for the visit and the medication. When they returned from the clinic, Mwezi had his suitcases packed and was ready to continue his studies in Belgium. Uncle Moyo and Mwezi hugged good-bye.

Esy prayed that the medication would help Moyo because she heard his wretched cough during the night. She hoped the next time she would see him he would feel better. She gave him a long good-bye hug and wished she had more money to help him out of his predicament, but she had to save more money. Also, the commitment she had to her son was at the top of her list.

The long good-bye hug she gave Moyo was the last. She received a note from her father that Moyo had died of pneumonia, which is a common complication of HMLD. Esy was heartbroken and bitter. She raged at her father's selfishness. *I don't understand why he couldn't help his only son.* In that note, Daddy Dayana asked her to help him with Moyo's funeral. He planned to bury him next to Mama. It was only six months after their last visit, so she reflected on the last Christmas Day with Moyo. It was hard to say good-bye. She reached for her mother's journal to comfort her.

My Dearest Esy,

Life is hard in the Congo, but love is never in short supply.

"*Love is patient, love is kind. It does not envy, it does not boast, it is not proud. It does not dishonor others, it is not self-seeking, it is not easily angered, it keeps no record of wrongs. Love does not delight in evil but rejoices with the truth. It always protects, always trusts, always hopes, always perseveres. Love never fails.*"
(1 Corinthians 13:4-8)

My dear Esy, remember — LOVE NEVER FAILS!

Love,

Mama Mary

ℭℜℭℜℭℜ

Preparing Moyo's funeral reminded her of all the heartaches they shared during their childhoods. Both were young children when they lost their mother. Their family couldn't afford a doctor for consultation or treatment. They still didn't know what Mama Mary actually died of, because a doctor did not treat her. Esy thought it might have been an STD. In many ways they lost their father at the same time, too. He just wasn't the same person after she became ill. The evils of gambling grabbed him by the throat and pulled him to forbidden places. They were both strong Kimbanquists, but life ensnared and defeated them.

Esy recalled how Moyo ran to get her from the mine to let her know that Mama was dying. At her bedside, the two of them kissed her, and listened to her words of advice one last time before she died. They clung to her until she breathed her last breath. Then, night turned to morning and they held her close long after she died.

Esy didn't walk to the little hut in the country—Russell drove her there and dropped her off informing her he would pick her up in two days. Those two days were filled with reverie, preparing food, and cleaning the hut since Daddy Dayana moved back in.

"Esy, how have you been?" Daddy Dayana asked.

"I'm doing well. I finished high school and am working as a translator for the governors of the mines. I'm sure Moyo mentioned that I have a son. His name is Mwezi Cox. He's at a boarding school in Belgium."

The bags under Daddy Dayana's eyes were pronounced and he had lost weight from the grueling work at someone else's bidding. This was the life Esy did *not* want and worked so hard to avoid. "How are you?"

"I'm getting weaker but more stubborn everyday," he said with a smile. "I hope to see you more often."

Esy knew that wouldn't happen. His life was entangled with his "friends" and the gambling he did with them. Her feelings about her father remained flat. Nothing ever changed.

Moyo's funeral procession was much like Mama's. The beating of the drums called the mourners together. Grief wailing and deep sobbing filled the air surrounding the little hut. After that, they celebrated the cycle of life by eating, singing and dancing. Moyo was given a proper burial so he could happily join the spirit world. His remains were buried in the red earth under the Baobab tree next to Mama.

CHAPTER 9

The Apartment

CRCRCR

The colonel's brutal attack left its mark on Esy. She remained incontinent. Every time she changed pads, she cursed the colonel and Hackett. She had some control, but not enough to regain her confidence. So many dreams had been destroyed during that horrible ordeal. Finding a husband or intimate partner seemed impossible. She could feel her heart twist when young men would flirt with her. She'd play along for a while, then she would grow angry at the situation and push them away. She built an impenetrable shield around herself. Closeness with men, especially those who wanted something from her, was nearly impossible because she didn't trust anymore. She only trusted Russell because he had signed a contract and agreed never to touch her again.

While on the outside she was still an attractive, athletic young woman, on the inside she was someone scarred and ashamed of her injuries and limitations. Falling in love and having a family meant becoming vulnerable.

She feared humiliation and shame. After her experience in the brothel, did she even want intimacy? In her private moments, she harbored resentment toward men.

Who could she blame for her dreadful predicament? Was her father to blame? After all, if he hadn't forced her to work in the mine, she never would have met Hackett. She could have enjoyed a simple life in the little hut with her mother and Moyo. Maybe Hackett should be blamed. He viewed her through the eyes of a predator homing in on her weakness and tempting her with it— dangling the promise of an education in front of her.

Could Stella be blamed? If she hadn't schemed for a baby, Esy's life would have stayed on track. And after Mwezi was born, if Stella had kept her promise of caring for Mwezi, Esy wouldn't have gone back to the mine to scrape out a living. This put M at risk for lung disease, which forced her to work for Hackett. Hackett didn't care about her or protect her, which led to the colonel's hateful retaliation of Hackett's political agenda. Esy was the helpless victim caught between two evil misogynists. She was the innocent carnage of their ire. The colonel's butchery destroyed her body. These circumstances demolished her future ...evil and hate must take the blame.

Hate soured her insides. She held men in contempt and anyone who exploited others for their own gain. *And then, there was Russell—I think he was a coward. He allowed himself to be manipulated by Stella.* Those thoughts stalled Esy's litany of blame. She reflected. *Maybe he is the exception? He wanted Stella to be happy. Was he being loving in his own way? Russell apologized to me for his behavior and Stella's behavior. He said he 'would never touch me that way again' and Russell has been true to his word. He's a good Daddy to Mwezi and that's important to me.*

My relationship with Stella has changed too. She still drinks too much alcohol and sleeps a lot, but she has kept her promise. M respects her because she took care of him when he was sick with that hacking cough. I knew M would get the best care so I could attend my classes without worrying about him. She gave me the opportunity to finish my secondary education. Maybe that's how she showed her love.

Still, I am her servant. She tells me what household duties to do. As her servant, I can't criticize her even when she treats M like he's her baby. I cook dinner for them every night and pay for M's clothes and spending money even though Russell has graciously paid his tuition. They have been good to M and me. We've made a good family of two moms, a dad, and a son. We have been a supportive team. We love and care for each other.

Her thoughts would twist and turn dark when the evil of that fateful night seeped into her soul. In that state of mind, she assumed everyone possessed unquenchable appetites that shaped their selfish intentions. Unchecked evil terrified her.

I need to be able to recognize love. It is as important as avoiding evil. She said it again to herself. *I need to be able to recognize love. It is as necessary as avoiding evil.* These thoughts were an epiphany for her. She said those words over and over. *I need to be able to recognize love. It is as important as avoiding evil.*

She became aware that Stella and Russell were different. It was as if a fog lifted and she could see the sunshine. Although imperfect, Stella and Russell loved her and M. This insight made her heart ache with love and she wept. What was this surge of emotion? Where did it come from? Perhaps it was the deep respect Esy had for Stella and Russell. She appreciated their kindnesses, and cherished their love.

God heard Esynama's cries for help and answered her prayers. In that moment her anger dissipated and made her free and liberated. She hadn't forgotten all that Hackett and the colonel did, but at that moment, the "anger-monster" stopped eating her up inside. Her anxiety quelled as she breathed deeply. Grace and gratitude washed over her and revived and energized her. Esy thanked God for her son, Mwezi. He gave her a reason to live. Even if she never married and didn't have more children, it would be okay. M fulfilled her need to love and be loved.

ભ્ભ્ભ

With Mwezi in his last year of boarding school, she decided she would look for an apartment in the city of Lubumbashi. It was time for her to become independent. She could afford an apartment that was about five hundred Zairean zaires, which was the currency established by the Mobutu regime. Her financial means dictated where she could rent. The business centers and the high-rise apartments dominated center city. In a more run down area of the city, broken cars with missing wheels and parts lined the apartment buildings, which was ravaged by theft and other crimes. The constant worry of victimization created stress for the people that lived there. Although the pit fires in the road were extinguished, it left ugly scars on the bumpy landscape. Esy shunned those areas. It was most likely the second tier outside of the city's core would be within her means, yet away from the high crime areas.

She walked and walked, determined to find something better. As she approached the Kafubu River just south of the industrial quarter, she caught sight of a well-kept three-story apartment building. The front lawn was manicured, almost park-like. There were a few parking places in front occupied by cars that were complete—with no stolen or missing parts and the outside of the building looked promising.

Esy needed a large room with a kitchen and at least one, maybe even two bedrooms. She liked the location because bus transportation to center city was nearby. Best of all, each apartment had a deck overlooking the river. She envisioned herself having breakfast on a small table, watching the ducks and other birds land and take flight. It would be entertaining, like watching a movie.

An older lady with a cane in hand answered Esy's knock on the office door. Door ajar, she scrutinized Esy, her eyes wizened and piercing.

"How can I help you?"

"I'm looking for an apartment to rent," Esy said. "Do you have one available?"

"Yes, I do. Would you like to see it?"

"Yes," Esy said.

"I'll get the keys."

Esy followed the old woman, who hobbled slowly. They walked the length of the apartment building along the yellow terrace. All the doors were painted orange. The captivating smell of gardenias saturated the air. Some apartments had beautiful potted flowers placed by the front door welcoming visitors while other doorways were plain. The elderly lady wobbled on unsteady feet as she climbed the stairs to the third floor. At the top of the stairs, she unlocked the door, shoved the door open with her shoulder, and let Esy precede her inside.

The apartment had one large room, which was a combination kitchen/living room. *So far, I like what I see.* There were also three small rooms positioned along the length of the hallway: two bedrooms—but one so tiny it could have passed for a closet—and a bathroom just like the one in Stella's house. She had grown accustomed to modern toilets, so this was a pleasant surprise.

"How much is the rent for this apartment?"

"It is six hundred and twenty-five Zairean zaires," she said flatly.

Esy felt her throat tighten. She found it hard to speak. "All I have is five hundred." Seeking a solution, Esy asked, "Am I allowed to have a roommate?"

"Yes, you can have someone living with you. That's very common."

"I'll let you know before the end of the week if I will take it," Esy said.

"Okay."

"By the way, what's your name?"

"My name is Sophie. What's yours?"

"My name is Esynama. I'll let you know as soon as I can."

Esy felt downhearted. The apartment was beyond her means. She decided to visit Hilda to see if she might want to be her roommate. This would be a good solution. Sharing expenses would allow Esy to save more money at the end of the month. Shifting away from being subservient was proving harder than she thought. *Gaining my independence is more work than I anticipate and supporting myself financially is challenging.* Being a servant girl was like a gravitational force trying to pull her back into its grasp. In some ways, being that way was easier. Yet, Esy was convinced this was the right time to climb out of that role and be free. Somehow, she was determined to make it work.

ᬇᬇᬇᬇ

Esy walked back through the center city to get to the house where Hilda worked. The outside of the house was the same, but the amount of people inside had changed. It was no longer a quiet little house as she remembered it, but a noisy one on the outskirts of town. One short knock and the door opened to a raucous gaggle of girls dancing in the kitchen. Boom boxes blared. The girls turned the volume down and stopped chatting when Esy entered.

"Is Hilda here?" Esy asked.

"She doesn't work here anymore," one of the girls, shouted.

"Where is she?" Esy asked, surprised.

"Anyone know where she is?" One of the girls bellowed out over the jibber-jabber.

"She left her address by the phone in her old bedroom."

"Why do you need her address?" another girl asked.

"I used to work here with Hilda," Esy said. The girls became very quiet. They turned the music off.

"You used to *work* here?"

"Yes."

"How long ago?"

"Almost fifteen years ago."

"What was it like back then?"

"There were only two girls working here, Asha and myself. Hilda was the house mother."

"You know Asha?

"Yes, she's my friend. I haven't seen her since she moved away."

"She's one of the Filles Londoniennes in the biggest and best hotel in Kinshasa," the leader of the group said.

"Has she been back for a visit?" Esy asked.

"Yes, just last month."

"I'm sorry I missed her. When I have my new address I'll share it with you. Please let her know that I would like to see her again," Esy said.

Another girl gave her a piece of paper with Hilda's address. Esy slipped it into her pocket and said good-bye. As soon as she walked out of the house, they turned up the music and started dancing. It was loud. *I don't know what a Filles Londoniennes is. I'll ask Hilda when I see her.* The next day, Esy was determined to find her friend, hoping she might be her roommate.

ೞೞೞ

Esy looked at Hilda's phone number and address on the slip of paper she received the day before. The address was familiar. She headed back to Stella's house to use the phone.

"Stella, could I use your phone?"

"Sure. Who are you calling?" she asked.

"I'm calling Hilda."

"Who's Hilda?" Stella asked.

Esy didn't answer her right away. Stella would not understand their complicated history and Esy didn't want to explain. "She's an old friend."

"From school?"

"No, from the time I worked for Hackett in the brothel."

"Oh no! Are you thinking about working there again?" Stella asked.

"Don't be silly. I will never, never work there again."

Esy could tell that Stella wanted more information. She might be sensing a major change in the works. "I'm looking for a roommate."

"A roommate? Are you planning to move out?

"Yes, I have found an apartment by the Kafubu River. I need a roommate to share the expense. It costs a lot of money." Esy walked away from the conversation, and slipped around the corner pulling the cord as far as she could. She didn't want Stella to overhear her conversation.

"Hello," Hilda answered.

"Hi, Hilda. This is Esy."

"It is so good to hear your voice. How are you doing?

"I'm doing well. How about you?"

"I walked away from my work as a house mother. The girls are unruly. Things have changed so much since you worked there."

"Do you have time for a visit today?" Esy asked.

"Yes, I would like to spend time with you."

"I have your address and I noticed it was near the school, Ecole International."

"Yes. I'm living with my sister Frieda. Do you remember her? It's only temporary since we don't get along very well."

"I do remember your sister. Would this afternoon be a good time?"

"Yes, I'm looking forward to it."

"See you soon. Good-bye, Hilda."

Esy turned her thoughts to Stella, who had gone to her room. Sometimes the fear of being alone and abandoned would set off Stella's drinking binges. She would have to talk to her about it. Wrestling with the responsibility she had toward Stella, Esy summoned all the compassion and love she had for her before she knocked on her bedroom door.

"Stella? Are you okay?"

There was no answer. Esy knocked again, but still no answer. She opened the door and walked in. Stella was in bed with her back to the door. Esy approached the bed and sat next to her. She hugged Stella and felt the cool of Stella's teardrops landing on her hand.

"Stella. I love you. You have kept your promise and our son is all raised and doing well. Thank you for everything you've done. I'll be back to visit you and Russell."

Esy almost said that she would make dinners for her but something stopped her. She did not want to be sucked into that servant role again. She wanted to be Stella's friend, *not* her servant. It took all her mental fortitude and intention to keep that from happening.

"I love you too, Esy. You have been a wonderful part of our family life. I have one request."

"What is that?" Esy asked.

"When Russell is out of town, would you come to church with me?"

"Yes, I would like that. You'll have to let me know, so keep in touch."

"I will," Stella said, as she sat up and gave Esy a long hug.

ରେଇରେଇରେଇ

Frieda had a lovely home in a pleasant part of town. As Esy was about to knock on the door, she heard Frieda's husky voice shout, "Did you talk to the banker about the check that came in the mail?"

"I told you that I would do it next week!" Hilda snapped back.

Hilda and Frieda were arguing. Esy let the squabble die down before she knocked on the door.

"Hello, Esy," Hilda said opening the door. "This is my sister, Frieda."

"Hi, Esy. Do you remember me?"

"Yes, I do. It's because of you that I finished my high school education. Thank you." Frieda reached out and they shook hands.

"I have a meeting, so I have to leave, but it's good to see you," Frieda said, as she walked out the door.

Once they were alone, Hilda said. "It has been a long time. What have you been up to?"

"I've been translating for a while now. Once I finished high school, I started working for the governors in the mines. When I wasn't translating, I cooked and cleaned for the Cox family. If I needed more money for M's spending money, I worked at a restaurant in Lubumbashi. The years after meeting you have gone by quickly. It's hard to believe that it's been almost fifteen years."

"Are you making more money from translating?" Hilda asked.

"Yes, it pays well and I'm getting more and more projects from the governors of the mines. I want to be independent, so I'm planning to move out of the Cox home. When did you quit working for Viktor von Peters?"

"That's a long story. I quit about three months ago. One of the girls punched me in the face. It has mostly healed now, but it scared me. Some of the girls that live there are nice, but a couple of them are vicious. Viktor paid me very well, but he's trying to make more money by adding more girls. That creates problems. Also, the police are enforcing the laws, too. Brothels are illegal, you know."

"It was a good time for you to quit. You'll save yourself some heartache." Esy said.

"I agree. So, you're moving. I wondered when that would happen. You have done so well. You finished your high school education, Mwezi is all grown up, and you've been able to make more money."

"I have one problem," Esy said reluctantly. "I can't afford the six hundred and twenty-five Zairean zaires for the rent, *but* I can have a roommate to help me with the cost."

"Oh, now I know why you came. You want me to be your roommate, right?"

"Yes, I do. I would enjoy living with you. We've done it before."

"Well, Frieda and I don't get along well. She's bossy, just like our dad was."

Esy chuckled as she recalled the argument she overheard between the two sisters.

"Let me think about it and I'll call you tomorrow."

જીભજીભજીભ

Hilda didn't call until noon. Esy was impatient because she wanted the apartment so much. It would be perfect for her and Hilda.

"Hi, Esy," Hilda said. "If I like the apartment, I will be your roommate."

Esy was so excited to hear that answer, she could hardly speak. "That's wonderful! I'm going to catch the bus over there as soon as I can and pay the first month's rent."

"Wait, wait! I want to see it first," Hilda exclaimed.

"Then I'll meet you there in about an hour. It's located east of the city of Lubumbashi and the route you take is Route de la Munama. It's near the bus stop by the South Industrial area. I'll meet you there."

If it were up to her, Esy would have been there in less

than an hour, but she could not control the speed of the busses. Time in her country was elastic—give or take a few hours. She *had* to learn patience. A one-hour trip turned into a two, almost three-hour bus ride. Hilda understood and calmly waited for her to arrive.

"Hi, friend. Let's get to this place. I'm eager to see it," Hilda said. The two of them walked quickly to the apartment building on the banks of the Kafubu River.

Hilda smiled when she saw the building. Esy knocked on the office door. Sophie opened it a crack and recognized Esy.

"You're back. And, who is this?"

"This is Hilda. I'm hoping she'll be my roommate. She wants to see the apartment before we pay the first month's rent."

"Okay, follow me. Oops, let me get my cane—I've got to climb those stairs."

The three of them chattered happily. Sophie climbed the stairs more easily than she had before and unlocked the apartment for the ladies. Hilda walked in first. She checked out the bathroom, the kitchen and the bedrooms.

"Who do we call if we have problems?" Hilda asked.

"First me, and then, I'll call the crew."

"When does the crew come and how long does it take?"

"Many of our men work for the industrial companies just north of here, so they live here and tend to our problems after work."

"That's convenient," Hilda said. "How about our rent? When is our rent due?"

"Always on the first of the month. There is a late fee after seven days." Hilda looked at Esy and nodded. "I want to talk with Esy in private," Hilda said.

The two of them chatted a bit and then they took one last look at the bedrooms.

"We're planning to move in on Monday," Esy said

"You'll have to prorate our rent because the first month won't be a full month," Hilda said.

"Yes, you will owe five hundred Zairean zaires today for this month."

"Very good," Hilda said. "We want a receipt showing that we've paid."

"Meet me at the office when you're ready. I'll have the receipt for you. Here are the keys."

Hilda was satisfied with the apartment. It was sufficient. "It's smaller than what I'm used to, but I like the location and the surrounding nature is pleasant," she said.

"The 'closet' is mine," Esy claimed with a smile.

CHAPTER 10

Imperiled

ରେଉଡ

It was moving day. Esy didn't have much, but what she had filled up the entryway of Stella's house. The phone rang, Stella got up to answer it.

"Hi, Stella. Is Mom there?"

"Mwezi?"

"Yes, could I speak with her?"

Stella handed Esy the phone, disappointed he didn't want to talk to her.

"I'm in Kinshasa right now," M said.

"What are you doing there? You're supposed to be in Belgium at school."

"I completed my exams and my friend and I flew to Kinshasa to join students from Lovanium University in a protest."

"Oh, no! Is that where the army killed students that I read about in the newspaper?"

"Yes, we don't know how many were killed because the army seized the bodies of the dead students and buried them in a mass grave. It's like they tried to make the dead bodies disappear."

"Are you alright? Are you injured?"

"I'm okay … a student died from gunfire about six feet from me."

"Oh, no!"

"Mom, I've never been that close to a dead body before. It was terrifying."

"Mwezi, come home right now!"

"My friend and I are at N'djili Airport. I've purchased a ticket to Lubumbashi. When I get there, I'll call you. I'll be home soon."

"Call Stella, I'm moving into my new apartment today." Esy looked at Stella who nodded.

"Good, I'll see the both of you soon," M said. "I love you, Mom."

"I love you, too."

"That son of ours—he gets into so much trouble." Esy's hands trembled as she put the phone back in its cradle.

"I'm just happy he's okay," Stella said.

She went downstairs for one last time. Patch was climbing the stairs towards her. It was Patch's way of saying good-bye.

"Hi, old friend," Esy said, as she reached for her. Sitting on the stair step she cuddled Patch. Memories of the silly chases around the corners of the house flashed through her mind. Patch had been her snuggle friend during the night. She pulled Patch closer to her and nuzzled the top of his head. "Please take care of Stella for me, okay?" Gently, she set Patch down and checked for anything she had left behind. She went through the dresser draws, the closet and finally, the bathroom. There was nothing there of hers. In M's room, however, there were lots of old clothes he had outgrown, combs and other grooming paraphernalia in the bathroom. She shut the bedroom door behind her, gave Patch one last nuzzle and climbed the stairs.

"I'm sure M will be tired when he arrives," Esy said to Stella. "Let him sleep in, and I'll stop by to see him sometime around noon."

She gave Stella a good-bye hug. "I love you," she said as she walked out the door.

ରେ ରେ ରେ

When M returned from Kinshasa, he shared unbelievable stories. No one knew how many protesters died, because the soldiers dug a big pit and got rid of the evidence. Mwezi's friend counted almost fifty. The army arrested close to eight hundred students and the judges who sentenced them were merciless, especially to the leaders of the protest.

"I remember someone yelling, 'Shots fired! Lie down! Lie down!' Which, of course, I did. My heart was pounding against my chest. I heard a moan of pain to my right and then, silence. It terrified me—a young student with so much promise died in an instant. I lay face down on the ground for a long time until others around me stood up and scattered looking for a place to hide."

The possibility that they could have lost Mwezi overwhelmed his family. Stella and Esy cried out and raised their hands, thanking God for his safe return. Russell hugged his son, reluctant to let go. He feared if he released Mwezi, he might never see him again.

"I'm happy to be home," M said. "I hate Mobutu and

his army. They are cruel and unjust. He needs to go. Life isn't fair and I *must* help make it fair."

"I know son. Life isn't fair," Esy said.

"The world needs to hear and to listen to the students!" Mwezi's restless soul stirred.

Following this horrific event, Mobutu's response to the carnage was still more brutality for the crime of disobedience. His regime punished protesters with torture and long prison sentences. Manifeste de la Nsele, a document espousing his views, became required reading in all the schools. It was clear that Mobutu's regime would only allow a one party system known as the MPR (Popular Movement of the Revolution).

Mobutu won the next election in 1970 with almost ninety-nine percent of the vote. Armed guards watched the voting process, which intimidated the people. They had to choose between a red ballot or a green one. Red represented a vote against Mobutu and bloodshed. The green ballot was the color of hope, manioc, MPR and a vote for Mobutu. In later elections, the slogan for the Popular Movement of the Revolution was, "Long live the three Zs! Zaire our money, Zaire our river, Zaire our only nation." It was not a unanimous election, however since there were one hundred and fifty-seven dissenting votes, all of them from the student district.

ಞಞಞ

"But, Dad, I want to go with my friends to protest this Zaïrianization. It doesn't make sense. When the industry is nationalized, Mobutu's friends will replace the experienced governors of the mines and they know nothing about how to run a mine. This will destroy our economy," M exclaimed.

"Son, sometimes in life you have to let things be. Mobutu is a powerful leader. He has brought hydro-electric power to this country, and many people have televisions in their home, especially in Kinshasa. And, the United States and Israel support him. He's driven to create a place for Zaire on the world stage and he does *not* let anybody stand in his way."

"Dad, do you think he's good for our country?"

"He's both good and bad. Removing the governors is a bad idea. It puts my job in question and jeopardizes my safety, but his military has kept order in this country."

"Why have you stayed in the Congo all these years? Do you like your job that much?"

"I'm good at my job, so the governor gives me freedom to travel to visit other mines here and abroad whenever I want. I like the relaxed life style in Africa. As you know by now, the Belgians are a regimented people. I don't fit there. I'm paid well here, *and you* are one of the reasons I stayed for so long," Russell said with a smile.

∞∞∞∞

Mwezi couldn't understand why his father wanted to let things be. For M, if you were unhappy with your country, you needed to say *and* do something. M was certain that chaos was coming, and it would be during his life-time. His father was just too old to care—he didn't have any fight left in him.

M's thoughts were conflicted. He had finished his secondary education, and he didn't know what to do next. Should he go to college at Université Catholique in Belgium or Louvanium University in Kinshasa? Perhaps he should get a job and make money—he was tired of being a student. He was sure of one thing, though—he didn't like what was happening with the economy in Zaire, especially in Lubumbashi.

M's best friend from his school days in Belgium was Samual Abara. Bright enough students, the two of them were teammates on the football team. They were at the same crossroads: what do we do now? The summer after graduation, M decided to visit Samual in Kinshasa. The reunion was happy one. From the first time they saw each other, it was as if no time had passed since they'd seen each other. They shared stories from school days and commiserated about their uncertain futures.

Samual's father, Noah, was a clerk at the Central Bank (Banque Nationale du Zaire) in Kinshasa. He harbored anti-Mobutu feelings because he saw first hand how Mobutu's policies were destroying his country. Noah witnessed businesses snatched from their rightful owners and usurped by the cronies of Mobutu under the guise of nationalizing industry. In one instance, Noah's boss ordered him to give liberal disbursements to Mobutu's cousins for a company they seized from a respectable, hard working family. Offended by the injustice, Noah refused to give them money. Outraged, Mobutu's relatives went to another bank.

At the end of Noah's workday, Dede, Samual's mother, made a delicious meal of fresh fish and manioc. The setting was just right for the men to share their views and most of the talk was about Mobutu and his foolish use of power. A forceful knock on the front door interrupted their animated and derogatory conversation.

Dede opened it and two armed guards forced their way in, violently pushing her aside.

"We have orders to find Noah Abara and take him to the police station for questioning.

"Oh no! Not my Noah," Dede wailed as she tried to shield her husband from the belligerent guards.

"Get away, woman," the guard yelled. He wrenched Noah away from her, turned him around and threw him against the wall.

"He has done nothing wrong! Why are you doing this to a good man? He's my father!" Samual shouted and hit the guard on the head. The other guard caught Samual and twisted and jammed his arm behind him. Samual cried out in agony, which inflamed Mwezi. Provoked by the hostility and injustice, M grabbed a chair and with all of his might pounded the guard who was torturing Samual. The first guard raised his pistol and shoved it into Noah's neck.

"Do as I say, or I'll shoot him," he yelled. "You, with the red hair—get yourself over to the door, hands in the air."

Mwezi obeyed. The guard tied his hands behind his back.

"You." He pointed to Samual. "Get over to the door, hands in the air." He tied Samual's hands as well and handcuffed Noah. The guards forced the trio into the vehicle at gunpoint and then took them to the police station in Gombe. Dede collapsed on the couch hands over her face, sobbing. Her heart ached, so worried she might never see her husband or her son again.

☙☙☙

The police station was a busy place. It was filled with "traitors" to the Mobutu regime. There was a putrid smell of unwashed, sweaty bodies. Of course, justice did not prevail—only the execution of harsh punishment existed. The fear in Noah's eyes betrayed him. He knew this might be his end. Mwezi and Samual slumped down, heads bowed, dreading the judgment that would come. They couldn't bear to look at Noah—it was too painful. The court handed out unfair judgments. One man, who owned a gas station didn't fill the gas tank of Mobutu's friend because he needed to fill his own tank. He was thrown into jail for two years. Another old gentleman refused to turn over his land to Mobutu's brother and he was sent to prison for life. Those waiting their turn became agitated fearing the outcome of their case. There was no justice in those cases, only vengeance.

"Noah Abara. Come to the bench. State your name and offense."

"My name is Noah Abara, and I don't know why I was arrested." He stood in silence, handcuffed, and flanked by two armed guards.

"It says here that you refused to disburse money from your bank to Mobutu's cousins when given specific orders to do so. How do you plead?"

"Guilty. What law did I break?"

"You disobeyed the policies of Zaïrianization. Take him away." One guard grabbed his arm and hastened him to the back room.

Samual and Mwezi looked up—sheer terror on their faces. Noah's eyes pierced their hearts. "Seek justice," Noah screamed between clenched teeth.

"Samual Abara and Mwezi Cox. Come to the bench. Why were you arrested?" The judge asked.

Samual talked first, "I was trying to protect my father. He is a good man."

"Mwezi Cox, why were you arrested?"

"I fought to keep my friend Samual from being hurt," Mwezi said.

"There are no report of crimes against the state for the these two men. You are released."

The armed guard untied them and permitted them to leave. They heard a shot from the back room. Once released, they sprinted to the back of the building and peered in the windows to find Noah. Where did he go? What happened to him? They scurried to the next window desperate to find him. He was not there. Then they saw the guards carry a limp lifeless body out from a back door and over to a cleared space outside. A moment later, they heard the whir of a helicopter, and watched helplessly, as the guards lifted the body into the chopper before it rose into the air. The slap of the rotor blades cut through the night air sending shivers up Samual's spine. His fear was that the body they took away was his Daddy.

"That's my daddy. I know it is," Samual said.

"Let's see if we can tell where it's going," Mwezi exclaimed, as they followed the blinking lights of the helicopter in the sky.

The two young men exploded with an adrenaline rush, running as fast as they could after the helicopter. The chopper didn't travel far—just to the southern bank of the Congo River by the rapids, when it came to a hover. They saw the dark silhouette of a body being thrown from the helicopter into the rapids of the Congo River. M and Samual heard the splash as the body entered the water. They stopped running and looked at each other in panic. Noah's body would travel to the Atlantic Ocean if not eaten by crocodiles or devoured by a Tiger Fish first. It was unlikely they would ever find his remains. Samual sobbed with inconsolable grief. Mwezi did his best to comfort his friend. It wasn't enough—nothing would ever be enough.

CR CR CR

This horrific event shaped Mwezi's life. He would wake in the middle of the night wet with sweat from a recurring nightmare. The sounds of the helicopter, the splash in the water, the blast of the gunshot replayed over and over in his dreams. Noah's last words "seek justice" hounded him day and night. They echoed in the chambers of his brain and became his mantra. He wondered how he could seek justice in his life. He questioned any lifestyle that put himself before others. He was in a quandary and his future looked even more uncertain.

His thoughts drifted back to the judge and he became outraged by the hasty judgment and condemnation of Noah before they searched out the facts. It was a miscarriage of justice. The corrupt judge was playing the roles of judge, jury and executioner, and he was a puppet of the brutal Mobutu government. If this process had been fair, and the rights of the individual heard, justice would have been served. At that moment, Mwezi resolved to learn more about the criminal justice system. He was driven to be a fair judge and one that put justice above all else.

M spent the entire plane trip back to Lubumbashi contemplating what he should tell his parents. He knew his harrowing ordeal would upset them. M decided to share it with his mother and not his father. Since his Mother had been the victim of cruelty and injustice, he was certain she would understand. M was accurate in his assessment of his mother. Horrified by the injustice and the affect on her son, Esy fully comprehended the evil of the Mobutu government.

ঙেস্ঙেস

"Dad, I'm deciding what I want to do with my life, and I'm not sure what the next steps are," Mwezi said during an evening meal with Stella and Russell. He considered this home, and Esy's apartment as a place to visit and enjoy his mother's company.

"This is the time in your life to do that. Do you have a career in mind?" Russell asked.

"I want to be a judge, a good one who seeks justice."

"Not an engineer?"

"I want to learn more about criminal justice systems around the world," M replied.

"You'll have many years of study ahead of you, but you are a good student. To be a judge, you first have to be a lawyer, so you need a law degree. Your next step is to go to college, and I would suggest the Université Catholique in Belgium. It is the best school in that country and it has an excellent law school."

"Are you willing to pay for my education?"

"Yes, I'll pay for your tuition and books. You'll have to make money for your living expenses. Perhaps your mother will be able to help. Her apartment is expensive, but she's a hard worker, and makes a good wage."

"Thanks Dad, for listening. Your advice has removed a lot of worry."

CRCRCR

"A judge? A lawyer?" Esy questioned. "Why not an engineer like your father?"

"It's important to me to make a difference in this world—I want to seek justice," Mwezi said.

"That's admirable, Son."

"Would you be able to help me with my living expenses when I'm at the school?"

"I'm sure I can help, but I don't know how much I can spare. Being independent is more expensive than I thought. I'll know more in a month. Let me know how much you think you'll need."

"I'll be looking for a job soon so I'll make money too," M said.

M and Esy took a long walk together. Esy shared her trials of breaking away from being a servant and the difficulty of being independent. M shared his ongoing frustration with the Mobutu regime, and the length of time he would have to be a student. Esy listened intently and was pleased that he was making progress with his career path. The sun set and it was time to head back to her apartment to visit with Hilda. Mwezie and Hilda told jokes, and the night would not have been complete without a prank. Hilda brought out a plate of cookies with a plastic spider in the middle.

"What kind of ingredients do you put in these cookies, anyway?" M asked, laughing.

Mwezie slept on a cot in the living room, and Esy went to sleep in her "closet." Before she fell asleep she said, "Judge Mwezi Cox, I like the sound of that."

CHAPTER 11

The Announcements

ଔଔଔ

"Esy, Esy!" Hilda shouted. "You have a letter from Louvain, an impressive-looking letter."

Leaving the door ajar, she opened her eyes wide at Hilda's news. She reached out, curious, but examined the envelope with care before she pulled out the printed card tucked inside. It was an invitation to Mwezi's graduation from law school at the Université Catholique. A broad smile spread across her face as tears welled up in her eyes. Hilda knew it was a smile of satisfaction and tears of joy.

"I'm so proud of him," Esy said. "I *must* see M graduate."

"Is this your first trip to Belgium?"

"Of course."

"Would you like some help?"

"Yes, I have so much work to do before I can take time off for a trip."

"You have a month to get everything done," Hilda said. "I can help."

"Thank you, friend."

CRCRCR

Esy reflected on the past seven years when M was in college and then law school. Mwezi gave up the life of protest and went into the legal profession, so she knew he was on course for a successful life. These past years, in many ways, were golden years for Esy. They slipped away so fast—like a thief in the night. Her own career was progressing nicely, and the relationship with her roommate was going well. Living with Hilda was like having another wise mother by her side. Her own mother's journal continued to be helpful, guiding her through the obstacles of life. The most recent entry resonated with Esy and she dwelled on it over and over again in her mind. She resolved to overcome the servitude issue. It had bedeviled her for so long, and finally, she was doing something about it. The feelings of inferiority and helplessness in the face of dominance were ingrained; it was almost part of her DNA. She realized that others were not going to change, so she had to react to them differently by becoming more assertive and purposeful.

Dear Esy,

I know your independent spirit. I remember how adamant you were about dressing yourself and holding the book I was reading to you. You often said, "Mama me do it." So what I want for you, more than anything else, is for you to be free and independent. In my own life, my strongest yearning was to be liberated, to find freedom. I turned to the Kimbanguist religion. "It is for freedom that Christ has set us free. Stand firm, then, *and do not let yourselves be burdened again by the yoke of slavery." Galatians 5:1.*

Esy, you must keep working on becoming free—in your heart, in your mind and in your actions. Stand up to those who try to dominate you for their own gain.

Love always,

Mama Mary

How did Mama know I would work so hard to find my freedom? So much of being free is a state of mind. Esy recognized her tendency to wait on people, to serve them. She wanted to find a different way of relating, a level that was equal. Before, she was the "it" in a relationship, an object that other people used at their discretion. Too many times, people exploited her for their own selfish ends. After getting an education and establishing a successful career, she strived to change those behaviors. She found, though, that the mindset of freedom and independence was hard to sustain. However, with each passing day, the path to emotional freedom became clearer and more understandable. With persistence, she did rise above her circumstances.

ॐॐॐ

So much had happened before Mwezi's graduation from law school. Mwezi found student life challenging at times. Esy did her part by making sure he had enough spending money. Every month for seven years, she sent four hundred Zairean zaires to her son in Belgium. M would go to the bank and cash them in for French francs. Inflation had been out of control in Zaire especially during the distressful years of the Mobutu regime. The Zairean zaire, as a unit of exchange, became less and less valuable.

When Mwezi first started school, he would come home for Christmas and summer breaks and write a letter to his mother once a month or so. That all changed as he advanced through his education. Esy took the change in M's behavior personally. She engaged in an internal debate because of M's altered behavior. *Why did M stop writing me letters? I haven't seen him for two years, and he hasn't talked about coming home to see me. Maybe he's mad at me for not giving him more money. I wonder about how his schoolwork is going. I'll ask Russell if he has heard anything.* She brooded and worried about M so much it affected her sleep. She would wake up in the middle of the night wondering if she had done something wrong.

Her business as a translator paid well, but her income was uneven. She received payment only when someone engaged her to translate—feast or famine, as they say. Esy was an excellent translator and she became more fluent with each passing year. With experience, her confidence grew. Taking time off for M's graduation, and sightseeing in Belgium and maybe other parts of Europe would be a dream come true. It also meant she would have no income during her vacation. *Maybe I will ask Frieda if she knows of a student who could translate for me while I'm away. I would give the student translator a stipend and I would still have some money left over for myself.*

CRCRCR

The commencement invitation made her so happy, but M's silence agitated and worried her at the same time.

Perhaps Stella and Russell could give her some advice.

"Hi, Esy. Come in," Stella said. "How have you been?" Esy noticed how much Stella had aged. Her hair was thinner, her shoulders hunched over, and she had an awkward gait.

"Okay. Did you get an invitation to Mwezi's graduation?" Esy asked.

"No, but maybe Russell did ... Russell?" Stella shouted loud enough so he could hear her through the bedroom door. "Did you get a graduation invitation from Mwezi?"

"I haven't opened the mail for two or three days. The mail should be on my desk."

"Esy's here," Stella said. There was a rustling sound in the bedroom, and Russell opened the door.

"Hello, Esy," he said. "What brings you here?" Esy tried to hide her shock before she answered his question. Russell was unshaven, perspiring, and his red hair had patches of gray. She noticed a yellow pallor on his face and a slow shuffle as he walked to his desk.

"I received an invitation to M's graduation, and wondered if you received one too."

"Well, let me look," he said, as he sifted through his mail. "Yes, here it is." Russell took his time reading, a proud smile acknowledged the invitation. He looked up at Esy. "Our son has done it!"

"Do you think you'll go?" Esy asked. "I've been so worried about him because I haven't heard from him in over a year."

"Don't worry about him. Those exams are very hard. He's been devoting time to his studies. I don't know if Stella and I will go. It depends on how I feel."

"Have you been okay?" Esy asked.

"My doctor has been on me about my lifestyle. He says my heart and my liver can't take much more."

Stella, who was sitting quietly in a chair, stood up. "You'd feel better if you'd just follow your doctor's advice!" Then, she turned to Esy and said, "He's been drinking too much and he's never home. He flies from here to there. I never know where he is."

"I promised her I would stay home more," he said, averting Stella's eyes.

"Please take care of yourself," Esy pleaded. "You're very important to M and me." Esy walked toward him with open arms, looked into his eyes, hugged him tightly. Then, she hugged Stella. "I love you both very much. You are my family."

ભ્ર ભ્ર ભ્ર

Esy's next stop was to Frieda's office to inquire about a student with language skills to do her job while she traveled. As before, there was quite a wait to see her. Esy put her name on the list and took a seat. The wait was longer than usual.

After about an hour, a deep-throated voice said, "Esy, good to see you."

"Hello, Frieda."

"Come in," she said, and walked Esy back to her office. "How can I help you?"

"Mwezi is graduating from law school."

"Congratulations! So he *finally* did it! That's wonderful."

"Thank you," Esy said. "I need to ask a favor."

"I'd do anything for you and Mwezi."

"I want to go to his graduation ceremonies in Belgium,

but I can't afford the loss of income when I go on vacation. Do you know of a student that I can train to do my work while I'm gone?"

"What exactly do you do?"

"I'm a translator. When one of the governors of the mines gets questions or an order for one of the ores—cobalt, nickel, or copper—I translate the information mostly into French, but it depends on what each governor wants. The languages I translate are French, English, Kikongo, Lingala, Tshiluba and Swahili. Sometimes I do simultaneous interpreting, but that's mostly when guests come from the United States. Simultaneous interpreting is hard and tiring work. A student wouldn't be able to do that kind of translating. I'll make those appointments when I get back.

"So you need a student that is fluent in French and English and also has a good understanding of the different Congolese languages."

"Yes."

"I'll talk to the teachers and see what they can come up with," Frieda said. "I'll give you a call. I think you have the same phone number as Hilda, right?"

"Yes, I do. Thank you, Frieda," Esy said, as she shook her hand.

Esy was confident her trip would come together. There were so many pieces that had to fall into place. Just the thought of spending time with her son was exhilarating. The next step was finding a place to stay while she was in Belgium. And after that, she had to purchase a plane ticket. It would be so thrilling to fly for the first time ever. In her mind's eye, she had imagined it, but soon she would be faced with the reality of flying. *Maybe I can stay with M. I don't know where he lives or if he lives by himself or with a group of men. Does he have a spare bed? Does he have a place to cook food? I know I could sleep on the floor or on a sofa. I've done that before. M and I had to be flexible and tolerant because of all the moves we had to make when he was young. Russell is the one I should call since he has been to visit to him several times. He would know.* Thinking about the plane ride made her fearful. She would have to replace fear with a healthy anticipation. Without a doubt, there would be adventures in her future.

છઠ્ઠ છઠ્ઠ

Esy called Russell first thing in the morning. "Hello Russell, this is Esy. I'm planning my trip to Belgium. When I'm there, I'll need a place to stay. Does M have a place for me to stay in his apartment or does he have other people live with him?"

"No, he doesn't have roommates." Russell said. "But Esy, remember who you are! *You* are his *mother.* I'm sure he has a place for you at his apartment. Just let him know when you will arrive and how long you will be staying with him."

"Okay, thank you." Esy hung up the phone and just shook her head. She remembered her resolve not to think like a servant anymore. She still had inferior feelings about herself that surfaced when she was stressed or in a new situation. *I must keep working to overcome those feelings. I have so much to remember.*

Esy had never ordered plane tickets or asked for flight information before. She was unsure how to proceed and waited until Hilda came home so she could ask for her help. She mistakenly thought she would travel by Air Zaire Airlines to get to Belgium.

"Hilda, would you purchase tickets for me to Brussels from N'djilli Airport?"

"You will need to buy two airline tickets because you have to go to Kinshasa first. You'll have to buy a ticket through African Air Charter in Lubumbashi and then, buy a ticket from Kinshasa to Brussels. I can make the phone call. What day do you plan to fly and on what date do you want to return home?"

"I want to get to Louvain at least a day before the graduation ceremony which is on Saturday, May 23. I should fly out of Lubumbashi a couple of days before, on Thursday, May 21 so I can get a plane from Kinshasa to Brussels."

Hilda expertly found the right flights from Lubumbashi to Kinshasa and then, made a reservation for a connecting flight on Air Zaire to Brussels. Esy was relieved that Hilda helped her navigate the maze of purchasing tickets. All she had to do was wait for the tickets to come in the mail. She wrote to M and gave him the dates she would visit him at his apartment, her flight number, and the plane's estimated time of arrival in Brussels.

Next, she needed to train her substitute. Fortunately, Frieda called to set up a meeting between Esy and a student good at foreign languages. After meeting Elle, Esy agreed to train her. She would give her a stipend for the translating work she would perform while she was on vacation. Teaching someone her craft was something Esy hadn't done before, so she talked with Hilda about some teaching strategies that would work. Hilda was such an effective teacher when she worked for Hackett. Maybe some of her methods would work for her.

When the time came for Esy to travel, packing her suitcase was an all day affair. She packed sweaters, blouses, slacks, a light coat, pajamas, toiletries, and a lovely dress for the flight and the graduation. Esy remembered how she looked in the mirror when she bought her dress. Before her in the mirror was a thin, work-worn, forty-year-old woman. Her body was still athletic, but the UTIs, the consequences of her brutal attack had taken their toll. Esy's hair was frizzier and harder to manage and her skin drier, but her eyes were still a lovely deep brown color. They sparkled, especially when she was happy. She had to admit, they were her best asset. Esy found an orange dress and held it up to her eyes to see if it complemented them. *I like that! I look young and alive. I'll buy this one*, she thought.

More than anything, Esy wanted to buy an instant camera, so she could take pictures of M and have someone else take pictures of her with him at the graduation ceremony. She went to a local trading company to check on the price and decided the camera was too expensive. After buying the airline tickets and saving money for M's graduation gift, she had no money left.

Hilda inspected her luggage to make sure it wasn't too heavy for her to carry through the airport.

"Do you have a raincoat or an umbrella?" Hilda asked. "It can be rainy in Belgium during the springtime."

"No, I don't."

"You can use my umbrella. Do you have a camera?"

"I'd like to buy a camera—one of those Polaroid Instant Cameras, but I don't have the money for it. It's too expensive."

"Well, I think you have everything you need for your

trip in your suitcase." Hilda said. Esy planned her bus trip to the Lubumbashi Airport with mounting excitement. This was a dream come true. The phone rang.

"Hello, is Esy there?"

"This is her."

"Esy, Russell here. Hilda called and said you were shopping for a camera for your trip. I want to buy one for you. What kind do you want?"

Russell's offer left her speechless. A single tear ran down her cheek, the overflow from a grateful heart.

"Are you there?" Russell asked. "Did you hear me?"

"Yes, I'm here," Esy whispered. "I appreciate your kindness. Thank you."

"What kind of camera do you want?"

"A Polaroid Instant Camera."

"I'll bring one over tonight. You're leaving in the morning, right?"

"Yes, I'm taking the morning bus to the airport."

"Okay, I'll bring one over this evening."

ѹѹѹ

Now, Esy had everything she needed for the trip. Her suitcase was packed and Russell brought over the Instant Polaroid Camera. She slipped the camera into her purse along with the directions on how to use it. The manual would give her some reading material on the plane. Esy asked Russell if he and Stella were going to the graduation and he told her they would not be going because of his health. Esy was on her own. She wore her new dress and high heels for the flight. Excited, and looking forward to an adventure, she had to admit she looked well groomed and stylish, like a bon vivant.

After weeks of anticipation and planning, it was time to go. Hilda put on her jacket and walked to the bus stop with Esy. As the bus pulled-up next to them, they hugged and shared good-byes. Then, Esy boarded the bus that would get her to the Lubumbashi Airport.

Lubumbashi was the second largest city in Zaire, so its airport was very busy. The distance between the capital city, Kinshasa and Lubumbashi was more than fifteen-hundred kilometers, which meant a two-to-three-hour flight between the two cities. Esy went to the airline counter, had her suitcase weighed and checked. All she had was her coat and purse. She hoped her suitcase would be in Brussels when she got there. After finding a comfortable seat to sit and rest, she went into deep reverie.

When I was a young girl living with Mama, I would never have expected the experiences I've had. I toiled under the hot sun in the cobalt mine, was haunted and hunted by a predator, survived a near fatal knifing by a monster, and lived through three regime changes in the Congo. I also experienced the selfless goodness of Mary Ann, David, Hilda, and Asha. The joy of the love I feel for my son Mwezi, and the transforming reconciliation between myself and Stella and Russell are all good memories. And now, I am flying in a plane to Belgium to see my son graduate from law school. Mama would be amazed.

"Flight 238 to Kinshasa will depart from Gate 5," a mechanical voice announced over the loudspeaker. Esy followed the crowd to the gate and waited … and waited some more. She worried she wouldn't make her connecting flight to Brussels. To pass the time, Esy people-watched until the gate became active and a line started to form. Her heart pounded and it brought back memories of riding on an elevator for the first time. She could hear the roar of the engine and the chatter of the stewardesses. She followed the line onto the airplane, matched the number on her ticket with the seat number, and settled into her space, which was next to a window. She rubbed her hands together and forced herself to take a couple of deep breaths as she closed her eyes. She popped her head up and opened her eyes wide as she felt the engines rumble under her feet. She looked out the window to see someone testing the ailerons, making sure they were working correctly.

The plane became crowded with people who stashed carry-ons in the overhead bins. The stewardesses reminded the passengers to fasten their seatbelts as the pilots readied the plane for takeoff. Esy sat by the window next to two men; one was settling into a nap and the other reading *It* by Stephen King. Esy was fully engaged, aware of any change in sounds and air pressure in the cabin. She didn't know the reasons for all the different sensations, but she enjoyed the adventure of her new experience.

The plane proceeded down the runway, slowed and turned until it got clearance. Then the engine and propellers ramped up to full speed, vibrating the plane. Rolling faster and faster down the runway, at the right time, the plane lifted off and was airborne. It was a thrilling moment, but nothing compared to the quick change of the landscape from large to small, smaller and even smaller. With a clear view for miles, Esy could see the cobalt mines, like pockmarks on the countryside. The miniature cities and the surrounding bush lands shifting into thick, dark green jungles softened by the overhanging clouds. It was magnificent and awe inspiring. Then, the landscape changed to ribbons of parched earth with small patches of vegetation and watering holes perfect for animal habitats. The Congo was an untamed and spectacular land. Her eyes followed the curves of the Lualaba River, the Sankuru River, the broad Kassai River, and finally, the mighty Congo River, which wound its way into Kinshasa, the capital city. The three-hour trip passed quickly, opening up new horizons for the first-time traveler.

Esy fretted about her connecting flight. What would happen if she missed the connection? Several Air Zaire airplanes parked by the airport inspired confidence. She hoped one of the planes was there for her flight. She soon discovered, however, that her plane was delayed and had a late arrival time. It was almost an hour before she could board the plane heading to Belgium. The newness of flying had worn off, and the sun was setting, so Esy was ready for a long nap.

ଔଔଔଔ

Esy slept off and on during the nine-hour flight. She woke up just in time to see the lights of the city of Brussels, concentrated in the city center. Groggy from intermittent sleep, she rubbed her eyes to make sure everything was real and that the blast of light was still there. The gentleman sitting next to her saw her looking down.

"That's the Grand Platz," he said. "Have you been there?"

"No, I've never been out of Zaire."

"That is something worth seeing if you have time." They smiled at each other and then went back to their separate thoughts.

Esy loved M so much and was eager to see him. *I hope*

he's well. I wonder why he stopped writing me. Will he recognize me? Will he be there to meet me? What will I do if he's not there? She worried. As the plane landed, her excitement pushed her concerns away for a moment. Eager to see him and hug him once again, she resolved not to complain about his lack of communication for almost two years.

She walked off the plane and into the airport and spotted him right away. Her heart pounded with excitement. She wanted to embrace him and never let go, but her sense of decorum overruled her deep desire. He was tall and slender, just as she remembered, but his hairstyle had changed. *I think he's a handsome young man even though I am somewhat partial.* He wore a tweed jacket, button-down shirt, and khakis—looking like a young lawyer. Standing close to him was a striking fair-skinned, blonde-haired young woman. *Does Mwezi have a girlfriend? That would explain so much.* M approached his mother with open arms. The undying love they had for each other was rekindled with that one embrace. It was so good to be close to each other again, and they had much catching up to do.

"Mother, I would like you to meet my girlfriend, Ankara." They shook hands awkwardly. "You can call her Esy," Mwezi said turning toward Ankara.

"Girlfriend? Mwezi, why didn't you tell me?" Esy said with a glint in her eye.

"Everything got so busy with school and then, spending time with each other. Also, we have a surprise for you back in the apartment."

"I hope it's a good surprise."

"It is, Mom. It is," Mwezi said. "Here come the suit-cases. Mom, what does yours look like?"

"It is light brown with dark brown stripes on each end." They scanned the stacks of suitcases until they found Esy's. "That's it," she said. M grabbed her luggage before Esy could and like a gentleman he carried it to his car. "Mwezi, is this *your* car?" Esy asked, as he opened the door.

"Yes, it is. It's a used Fiat Panda, but it works for four people. I wanted to get an Austin Healy, but that was *not* practical." That made Esy laugh—it brought back so many memories. M drove to the student apartments and parked his car. He jumped out, and opened the door for his mother. Ankara grabbed her suitcase and they led the way up the stairs to where they lived. An elderly lady opened the door to greet them.

"I think he's asleep for the night," she said.

"Good. Did he give you any trouble?" M said, as he reached into his pocket for money to pay her.

"Not at all. He's a good boy," she said. "Good night, Ankara."

"Good night."

"Something more than graduating from law school is going on around here," Esy said.

M and Ankara were all smiles. "Mother," M said, "Ankara and I have a son. He's eleven months old. His name is Isaac and we call him Izzy. He has red hair, like his daddy, and the color of his eyes is the same shade as his mommy's. You'll meet him in the morning. Izzy is a happy little boy, loves to play peek-a-boo, and laughs often. He crawls all over, but he's holding onto furniture and walking around the couch and the tables."

"That is just wonderful—I'm so happy it brings tears to my eyes," Esy said as she wiped the tears away and looked around for a tissue. "Does Russell know about Izzy?"

"Yes," M said. "He held him a couple of weeks ago. I wanted to surprise you when you came for my graduation so I swore him to secrecy. He said he wouldn't say anything and I know he kept the secret safe. I have to get to the University early tomorrow morning to get ready for graduation. Ankara will drop me off, and then come back to spend the morning with you and Izzy. The two of you can talk then."

"When can the you and I talk?"

"After the graduation ceremonies, we'll spend some time together," M said.

"It has been a full day," Esy said. "I'm tired and ready to go to bed."

"We have a pullout couch. Will that be okay?" Ankara asked.

"Sounds perfect—I'm so tired I could sleep on a bunch of banana leaves."

ଔଔଔଔ

In the morning, Esy heard M and Ankara quietly leave and then about a half hour later, Ankara came back by herself. The baby was still asleep. Despite all the new surroundings and excitement of the day, Esy felt rested. The thought of M being a father made her wake-up and smile.

"He's a good sleeper," Esy said to Ankara.

"Yes, he is," Ankara said. "You'll see why when he gets up. He's constantly moving."

"Do you go to school, too?" Esy asked.

"I have a masters degree in psychology from Kathholieke Universiteit in Leuven."

"Are you working in your field?"

"Yes, but only part time. I'm three months pregnant."

"Oh, my!" Esy said, as she covered her mouth in surprise. "Your family is coming fast. Are you doing okay? You have so much to handle with the baby, your schooling and your job."

"Yes, I'm doing fine—that's the advantage of being young."

"When did you and Mwezi get married?"

"Mwezi and I aren't married—we haven't done the paper work or the ceremony, but we've been living together."

"You've had so much going on in your lives," Esy remarked. "It explains why I haven't heard from M in almost two years. How did you meet M?"

"We met at a party in Leuven." Ankara said. "He had a wonderful sense of humor and he made me laugh a lot. He is a good man—you've done a good job raising him."

"I did the best I could," Esy said. "Time has gone by so fast. What are your plans after graduation?"

"I've been accepted into a doctoral program at Utrecht University. I'm passionate about research in psychology."

"What about M?"

"He hasn't told you?" Ankara said in disbelief.

"No."

"He's doing an clerkship at the International Court of Justice in The Hague," Ankara announced. "It's a coveted position with all expenses paid." Esy gasped. Her jaw dropped. She remembered how he was going to "seek justice" by becoming a judge. This news was almost too much to comprehend. *How was he able to do that? All this time he's been pressing toward his goal. I am so proud of him. He's got some of his mommy's drive.*

"Izzy's up," Ankara announced. They both heard cooing

and lively noises coming from the bedroom. "What do you want Izzy to call you?"

"Bibi," Esy said with a smile. "That's grandma in Swahili."

"I'll change his diaper, and bring him out so you can hold him."

Ankara and Izzy carried on quite a conversation even though his part of the conversation was Izzy cooing. Esy did hear her say, "Izzy, Bibi's here to meet you."

Esy dressed, tidied up the bed and waited—it seemed like an eternity.

ॐॐॐ

Red curly hair, blue eyes and light skin … Izzy was beautiful to Esy—so adorable. Her arms opened wide when she saw him for the first time, but he was not so sure. He tucked his head into Ankara's chest and peeked around to size her up.

"This is Bibi," Ankara said as she walked toward her with Izzy in her arms. She kissed the top of his head for reassurance. He looked up at Esy and gave her a charming grin. Esy's face melted into a smile and she opened her arms to try again. This time he accepted that she was his Bibi. She lifted him into her arms and her heart filled with joy.

"Nakupenda, I love you, Izzy." She said, as they sat in a chair together with Izzy on her knees facing her. She touched his hair, felt his soft face, and kissed his hands. "Mrembo, beautiful."

Izzy soon had enough of sitting still, so he wiggled off her lap to the floor. He crawled energetically to the other side of the room. Esy laughed at his quick movements. He stopped, turned around and gave her a mischievous smile. Esy joined in. She got on her knees to chase him and ducked behind a cabinet and popped her head out.

"Peek-a-boo-boo!"

Izzy responded with a squeal, hid behind a table leg, peeked around and went "oooo!"

They teased each other with sounds of fun and pure delight.

"All right you two, Bibi has to get ready for the graduation ceremonies and I have to nurse you before Alice, the sitter gets here."

"Would you take a picture of Izzy and me, first?"

"Do you have a camera?"

"Russell bought me a Polaroid Instant Camera," Esy said, as she pulled it out of her purse.

"How does this work?"

"Push this button, and wait. After the film develops, it will slip out here."

"Izzy, sit on Bibi's lap and smile," Ankara said, as she tried to coax more expression. "What sound does a train make? Choo choo!"

Izzy smiled and raised his eyebrows. They waited for the picture to develop. The picture emerging out of the camera fascinated him. Ankara took Izzy into the bedroom and fed him while Esy tidied herself. She looked splendid in her new dress and high heels.

ભ ભ ભ ભ

The graduation ceremony was an elegant affair. The stage was bedecked with spring flowers, the orchestra played dignified music, and the new graduates walked with solemn expressions single file down the aisle. For Esy, watching her son be part of the ceremony was the crowning achievement of her life. She had raised him under duress, suffering unbelievable hardships and tribulation. Her love and persistence proved fruitful. She expected the trajectory of his life and future generations to change for the better. Esy followed the group of picture takers and took as many photos as she could. Mwezi had turned out to be a handsome, caring, and aspiring young man. Esy was proud of him.

Following the ceremony, Esy took many pictures of Ankara and M together, and Ankara returned the favor and took a picture of Esy and M. They ambled around the grassy lawn and noticed an array of food and delicacies on tables by a fountain. Champagne toasts were everywhere, celebrating the event. The three of them formed a circle of joy imbibing champagne and eating the delicious food. Fellow students and professors stopped by to chat, shake hands and offer congratulations. With pride, M introduced Ankara and his mother, Esy.

"Mom, there is one place I would like you to see in Brussels before you leave. It's The Grand Place—it is so beautiful. Do you want to go?"

"Yes, very much. A gentleman on the airplane pointed out the lights in the distance and called it the Grand Platz. It sparkled radiantly in the night sky."

They gathered by the car and headed to Brussels' center city.

"Another name used for the Grand Place is Grote Markt, which is a Dutch name," Mwezi said, as he continued acting like a tour guide. "It has guildhalls, a Town Hall and the King's House and is considered one of the most beautiful squares in Europe. During WWII it served as a hospital. When the Germans invaded Belgium, they used it as a field kitchen. Now, it's an open-air market. Local merchants sell meat, bread and cloth and chocolates!"

"They have the most beautiful lace cloth and the best chocolates," Ankara said with excitement.

When they arrived, Esy thought, *yes, it is all M said it would be.* The buildings encircled the plaza area and in the center of the plaza were exquisite gardens of red, yellow, pink and blue flowers all arranged to perfection, like a structured French garden. It was beautiful. Esy snapped several pictures of the gardens with her Polaroid. Ankara found the candy store and bought some chocolates to share with Esy. Creamy and smooth to the taste, the sweets were scrumptious. Crystal chandeliers illuminated the lace and the handmade tablecloths. They were artfully displayed. Belgium fineries were so different from African ones. The earth tones, and wooden carvings of Africa were strikingly different from the white, shiny, pristine splendor of the Belgian wares.

"Thank you for showing me the market. It is beautiful," Esy said as they walked to the car.

"We have one more event planned for you," M said.

"Another one? What is that?"

"We would like you to attend our wedding."

"Your *wedding*!?" Esy exclaimed.

"Yes. Ankara and I have a small wedding planned in Leuven, where she went to school. We have a little church reserved for tomorrow at two in the afternoon."

"With all my heart, I want to be there. But, there have been almost too many surprises."

"There won't be a lot of people, just you and Ankara's parents. They are coming from Rotterdam. Alice will come too, so she can watch Izzy. We want him there, but he's so full of mischief—he would get all the attention," M said with a smile. Ankara and Esy laughed.

CRCRCR

So much had happened in Esy's short stay in Belgium—she had so much to think about and process. Esy couldn't sleep with all of the events swirling around her head. She wondered what Mama Mary would say about it all. *Education was so important to her. I know M's attainments would have pleased her. She would be as thankful and surprised just as I am. Mama's grandson has found his voice, and future generations will live a life of service to others by choice, not by the demeaning domination or the exploitation of others. Could it be that our family has risen above that kind of domination? Have we gained our freedom? That would be wonderful, if it were true. I wish I could see into the future.*

The next morning the Cox family climbed into the car and drove to Leuven, Belgium. It was a tight squeeze with M, Ankara, Alice, Izzy, and Esy as passengers. Ankara and M packed a lunch of cheese, fruit, bread, and wine for all of them. They found a park along the way and spread their meal on a picnic table.

The church was Sint Anthonius Kerk, a small Catholic church by a lovely neighborhood courtyard. Esy took pictures. She was grateful that Russell bought the camera. Ankara and M found dressing rooms in the basement, and a flower shop delivered fresh pink and white tulips and a fragrant vase of grape hyacinth. Alice entertained Izzy with Dutch rusks, and other teething biscuits. She kept him calm with walks in the courtyard.

Ankara's parents, Adriaan and Jeltsje De Jong met Esy, Alice and Izzy in the courtyard. Izzy recognized them at once and wanted Jeltsje to hold him. She brought a pocket full of treats and a bag of toys for him. Esy introduced herself and talked with Adriaan while Alice, Izzy, and Jeltsje played.

"I am pleased to have Mwezi as a son-in-law. He is a good and kind young man."

"Thank you," Esy said demurely. "I was overjoyed to meet Izzy and Ankara. She is a good mother and makes Mwezi happy and that makes me happy. They are good for each other."

The delicious aroma of the hyacinths greeted the wedding guests as they entered the chapel. The pink and white tulips on the altar gave the church a special charm. The priest invited the small gathering to sit together near the front and the music provided by the church organist created an atmosphere of reverence. Mwezi came through the door on the right and stood solemnly by the priest. Ankara came from the back of the church in a lovely, street-length dress with white sandals. A crown of white daisies adorned her long blonde hair and a cascade of white lace trailed down to her waist. She looked as pure and fresh as the first day of spring.

Mwezi cried tears of joy when he saw his lovely bride approach the altar. Izzy saw his daddy crying and held out his arms to go to him, to comfort him. M took Izzy in his arms and kissed him. Ankara joined M and Izzy, and at that moment, Esy took a picture with her camera, preserving that glorious moment for all eternity.

Following the ceremony, the bride and groom and the wedding guests had a Rijsttafel dinner catered in the church basement. The food presented was an unending parade of plates filled with some spicy, some sweet delicacies. It was the best Indonesian cuisine anywhere, and champagne flowed for the blessed family event.

CHAPTER 12

Deliverance

ભ્ર ભ્ર ભ્ર

Traveling back to the Congo took a long time. Esy felt nauseated, but concluded it might be her lack of enthusiasm for going back to Lubumbashi. She wanted to stay at Mwezi and Ankara's apartment and play with Izzy, but she had work obligations that needed attention. Esy wondered how Elle was doing with her clients, and there were two simultaneous interpretations scheduled she needed to complete. Hilda expected her, and would be eager to hear the details of her trip to Belgium. Esy was resigned to going back to her life as a translator.

By the time the plane landed in Kinshasa, Esy's nausea was noticeably worse, and was joined by an urge to urinate. She quickly sought the women's restroom. Nothing happened, and based on her past experiences, she self-diagnosed a UTI. It was uncomfortable at best and painful at worst. *I don't have time for this now. My life is too busy. I have too many obligations to fulfill.* She heard the loudspeaker say, "The African Air Charter service to Lubum-bashi will depart in twenty-two minutes at Gate 4." Esy quickened her pace and ignored the pains in her stomach.

Her European adventure had taught her how to sim-plify her carry-ons so she could stay organized. She had more items now than when she came—she had to buy a few keepsakes at the Grand Place. Her seat was in the economy section in the back of the plane near the tail. Esy saw this as an opportunity to take a nap, which she did for most of the flight. She woke when the plane landed at the Lubumbashi Airport. It was late at night, and so dark that she didn't relish finding a bus to navigate the streets of Lubumbashi. Finding a taxi seemed like the best plan to get to her apartment with all her luggage. She imag-ined herself as a world traveler now, and as someone who had more options to solve problems.

When they arrived at her apartment, the taxi driver lifted her luggage out of the trunk and carried the bags to her apartment door. Esy paid him, and the weary traveler sighed with relief when she opened the door. Hilda was waiting in the living room.

"Welcome home, Esy," Hilda said as she gave her a hug.

"Hi, Hilda. Good to see you, friend. It has been a long day."

"Let me carry your suitcases to your bedroom," Hilda said. "You look so tired. Are you feeling okay?" Esy shrugged and plopped in a chair. Hilda frowned and felt her forehead to check for fever. "You're hot. Where do you hurt?"

"I have a UTI, and haven't been able to go since I left Belgium."

"That's not good. I'm going to give you some aspirin for pain, and you must go to bed. I'll call the clinic when it opens in the morning."

Esy dragged herself to bed and slept soundly until morning. Hilda was bustling about the apartment when Esy woke. She had chills and a fever, so Hilda called the clinic to see what the wait time would be.

"There were so many sick people that came in yesterday. Monday was a bad day, so many high fevers," the nurse said. "There will not be any times open until Wednesday morning."

"We need to be seen sooner than that. She has a high fever and chills. We'll come down and wait," Hilda said. "Esy, let's go to the clinic. We can buy some cranberry juice on the way."

The two of them left to go to the store and then rode the bus to the clinic. There were more than fifty people sitting in the dirt along the outside wall of the clinic, waiting for their turn—mothers with their babies, old men with their heads tilted back against the wall, and whole families sleeping in the hot sun. Esy and Hilda sat and waited. The line moved at a snail's pace. Soon, they realized she wouldn't be treated until tomorrow, so they returned to the comfort of the apartment where Esy would not be exposed to the illnesses of people waiting in the dirt and hot sun.

The next morning, Esy was sicker than the day before. Hilda felt her forehead, and it was hotter than hot. Esy vomited. "We should call an ambulance," Hilda said. "It's very expensive, but they will take you right to the hospital."

"I spent all my money on my trip to see M. I don't have the money for an ambulance."

"Well, then let's get to the clinic early. Maybe you can see a doctor."

Hilda and Esy tried the clinic again and once again, they found dozens of people waiting to get treatment.

Many had waited over night to save a place in line. Esy had to lean up against the wall to catch her breath.

"I'll pay for the ambulance," Hilda said. "You can't go on any longer without medical treatment." The two of them returned to the apartment so Hilda could make the call. Esy was lethargic from fever, exhaustion, and pain.

CR CR CR

Esy could hear the ambulance coming up the street. She hoped that would mean relief from her nausea and pain. Hilda ushered them into her bedroom. The attendant took one look at her and ordered his partner to get a stretcher. He checked her pulse and felt her hot forehead.

"Mybaya homa," he said shaking his head. They placed her body on a canvas stretcher and carried her to the ambulance. Hilda insisted she would ride with them to the hospital. The trio squeezed into the front seat with Esy in the back of the ambulance. With flashing lights and a blaring siren, the driver drove them to the hospital. Once there, they whisked her through the back entrance to the emergency room. Hilda stayed right behind the stretcher. A nurse arrived to check her vitals. Discovering a low pulse and high fever, she called for a doctor.

"What's her status?" the doctor asked.

"She has a high fever and weak pulse and her companion says she's been vomiting."

"Esy's been ill for four days. We think it's a bad UTI. We went to the clinic Tuesday and Wednesday but she couldn't get treatment—the lines were too long," Hilda said.

"Esy, what have you done to treat the UTI?" the Doctor said.

"Water, cranberry juice," Esy whispered.

"Is that all?"

"She added lemongrass oil to her steamer, too. I gave her aspirin for pain," Hilda said.

"We'll have to give her antibiotics intravenously," he said. "Her body is working hard to fight a nasty infection."

Two nurses entered with a drip solution. They inserted a needle into the vein on her right arm and also gave her some pain medicine orally. Then, they left to care for other patients. Now it was the waiting game to see if the antibiotic would take effect.

"Hilda, I don't think I'm going to make it," Esy said. "My body is so weak. I have searing pain in my abdomen. It is worse than I have ever known."

"We have to give the medicine time to work," Hilda said reaching out to hold her hand.

"Please let Russell know I'm in the hospital. He can contact M and Ankara."

"Let's see how you feel in the morning," Hilda said. "I'm going home to get some sleep."

"I have a favor to ask. Mama's journal is under my mattress. Would you bring it to me when you come tomorrow?"

"I will. Do you want anything else?" Hilda asked. "You need to get some sleep, too. I'll see you in the morning." She stroked Esy's hand and kissed her on the cheek.

❧❧❧❧

The medication blocked much of Esy's pain, so she was able to think of other things, and began to review her life. She was fascinated by how sustained silence enhanced her memory. Esy sensed her mother's presence so keenly that she reached out, imagining she might touch her. She remembered childhood scenes; saw her placing the manioc roots on the windowsills to dry in the hot sun. She saw her in the kitchen making meals for her family, and outside washing clothes. Esy loved her mama. She saw her father high in the palm tree with a machete cutting loose the greasy palm nuts, and Moyo was there in her mind's eye playing under the Baobab tree. She loved her little brother, Moyo.

Esy's mind's eye turned to the bittersweet time with Moyo at Mama's bedside before she died … Mama holding Esy close so she could hear the whisper of her last breath. Mama gifted her a journal that shaped her life.

Esy's life turned dark after Mama Mary died. After the funeral, Daddy Dayana and Esy trudged to the mine. She spent unending days toiling in the mine, sifting through the slag piles and the pits, sluicing in the water ditches in a relentless search for cobalt. Lured by the promise of an education, she confronted evil trickery and savage brutality. Then, the faces of Stella and Russell appeared in her mind's eye—so confusing. They used her for their selfish needs but now, she enjoyed a relationship of true love and caring. Her life with them produced the purest relationship of all, the love between mother and son. That love propelled her to work, to finish her education, to strive for a better life. It was a human sacrifice, but the quest set her free from bondage. *I placed the torch in M's hand and he continued to press on for freedom and justice.*

Esy was embraced by inner peace knowing she had done her best. She fell into a serene sleep.

CRCRCR

Esy woke up early with throbbing pain in her abdomen— it was as if she was being stabbed over and over again. She flashed back to the night of horror and the vicious attack by the wicked colonel. She screamed. Two nurses burst into her room and checked her breathing and her pulse.

"The pain medication has worn off," the first nurse said. "I'll get more."

The other nurse checked her temperature, which was dangerously high. "I don't think the antibiotics are working." When the other nurse returned, she left to find the Doctor.

"Well, we have to try another antibiotic," the Doctor said. The nurses attached another bag, hoping it would make a difference.

Esy relaxed as the pain medicine began working. But when her breakfast came, she had no appetite. Just looking at the food nauseated her, but she tried to force down some liquid.

"You have some visitors," one of the nurses said. "Do you want to see them?"

"Who are they?"

"Their names are Hilda, Stella, and Russell, I think."

"Yes, they're my family."

"Good morning, Esy. Are you feeling any better?" Stella asked. "What did the Doctor say is wrong?"

"I have a nasty infection that's not responding to the medicine they're giving me," Esy said. "My body is so sick—I'm not going to make it. Russell, would you please contact M and Ankara and let them know I want to see them one more time?"

"Hilda called us last night and I've contacted M and they are on the way. They should be here tomorrow."

"Thank you. Hilda, did you bring Mama's journal?"

"Yes," she said as she gently placed the journal next to Esy on the bed."

"Thank you."

"You need to leave," the Doctor said. "She must be checked. Hopefully, there is improvement."

The Doctor left the room and after Esy's visitors left, the nurse came in to check her vital signs and reported back to the Doctor. "She's dehydrated and the fever is not coming down," she said.

The Doctor ordered another saline solution and more pain medication. "I need a blood sample as soon as possible. It appears to be septic shock."

The whole day was taken up with medical interventions, but nothing seemed to work. Esy's body was racked with fever and the pain subsided only when the pain medication was working. She struggled to stay alive. The chills, fluctuating heart rate, and the confusion distressed her. Sleeping or waiting for the next interruption were her only options. She lost track of time.

"When will tomorrow be here?" Esy asked the nurse.

"It's ten o'clock in the evening, so tomorrow morning will be here in eight hours."

The only thing she felt like doing was sleeping. Then, she felt a gentle stroke on her hand and opened her eyes to see M by the side of her bed.

"I love you, Mama."

"Mwezi, you're here. I wanted to see you one last time. I love you so much. Did Ankara and Izzy come?"

"No, Izzy is sick, but they send their love. They have good memories of your visit."

"Will he be okay?"

"Yes, he has the flu. He'll get over it."

"I have something for you," Esy said as she gave him Mama's journal hidden under the covers close to her heart. "This is a family treasure … my mama's journal.

It guided my life—cherish it and follow her wisdom, my dear son."

In less than a week this illness ravaged Esy's body. Her arms lay at her side, weak and lifeless. Esy's face was drawn with a yellow tinge, and her breathing was shallow. Overcome with sadness, Mwezi embraced her and listened for the whisper of her breath... listening until she breathed no longer. Tears rolled down his face as he held her. The nurse, respectful of the moment, quietly took the equipment off Esy's body and left. M sat up and reminisced about the good times and the harrowing times with her—grateful to have a Mother who loved him so much. He picked up the journal, opened it to the first page and read:

Those Who Are Dead Are Never Gone
By Birago Diop, a Senegalese poet

Those who are dead are never gone:
They are there in the thickening shadow.
The dead are not under the earth:
They are in the tree that rustles,
They are in the wood that groans,
They are in the water that sleeps,
They are in the hut, they are in the crowd,
The dead are not dead.

Those who are dead are never gone,
They are in the breast of the woman,
They are in the child who is wailing
And in the firebrand that flames.
The dead are not under the earth:

They are in the fire that is dying,
They are in the grasses that weep,
They are in the whimpering rocks,
They are in the forest, they are in the house,
The dead are not dead.

AFTERWORD

The time frame of this story is 1947-1987, a time of undue suffering. They endured three regime changes, which caused widespread killing and rape. And now, thirty-five years later, the Democratic Republic of the Congo is still plagued by severe human rights violations. In my estimation, the two most egregious violations involve wartime rape used to dominate and secure power and forced child labor in the cobalt mines denying these children an education.

Children are routinely forced to work in the mines to eke out a living for their families and are trapped by poverty because they are denied an education. Despite their wealth in natural resources, the mineworkers in the DCR are the poorest of the poor, earning a mere two dollars a day. The UNICEF estimated 40,000 African children work in the mines, many of them mining cobalt. The health risks for these children are menacing, fatalities and injuries common, and they are susceptible to Cobalt Lung disease, which is a fatal form of pneumonia caused by cobalt dust. James Conca, in his article, "Blood Batteries," in the September 26, 2018 issue of Forbes Magazine wrote that times are changing. OECD (Organization for Economic Cooperation and Development) drafted "guidelines for corporations on mineral supply chains." Tyler Gillard, legal advisor to OECD posed a question to Fortune Magazine: "Are consumers going to demand child-labor-free, corruption free electric vehicles? I think it is coming." At present it has been reported that China's Chamber of Commerce of Metals, Minerals & Chemicals launched the Responsible Cobalt initiative last year to bring companies together. These companies include Apple, Samsung, HP and Sony. Apple has taken the initiative to take one hundred teenagers out of the mine and teach them other skills such as sewing, carpentry, and hairdressing. This is being done in the city of Kolwezi in the DRC. These initiatives, although small, give hope for the emergence of humane mining practices.

Another severe human rights violation is the pervasive human trafficking, prostitution, and rape that is tormenting the DRC. It is considered one of the most dangerous places for women, and some have said it is "the rape capital of the world." Jana Asher, a renowned researcher on sexual violence toward women noted that almost 40% of women have experienced sexual violence in the DCR and when she asked a young man of sixteen and a member of the military, about his views, he said, "If we see girls, it's our right… we can violate them." This is frightening.

Denis Mukwege, who received the Nobel Peace Prize in 2018, in his acceptance speech cited horrific examples of sexual brutality. The first patient Dr. Mukwege saw at his new clinic was a woman who was shot in the genitals by a local military leader. He received no punishment because he terrorized the villagers who witnessed the crime. Dr. Mukwege has worked tirelessly demanding the courts prosecute rape as a crime. Because of all the political conflicts, the killings leave sixty to ninety percent of the women as single heads of households. They need to walk long distances to find resources for their family to survive, and this makes them vulnerable to sexual predators.

The United States Department of State on June 14, 2014 stated in an article, "Democratic Republic of the Congo Trafficking in Persons Report," stated that the DCR... "is a source and destination of trafficking for forced labor and forced prostitution, much of which is internal and perpetrated by armed groups in the eastern region of the DRC. The DRC is said to be the main regional source, from which women and children are trafficked in large numbers to sex industries in Angola, South Africa, Republic of Congo and western Europe, particularly Belgium. In addition to forced prostitution in refugee camps, many girls are forced into prostitution in tent, or hut-based brothels, markets and mining areas."

As citizens of the world, we have a long way to go, but the first step is looking at this harsh reality. It is my hope that education becomes mandatory for every child in the Congo, that Christian missionaries continue their good work, and the entrepreneurs who gain from the natural resources in the DCR continue to find ways to share the wealth with the people of the Congo.

ACKNOWLEDGEMENTS

I acknowledge the spirit of the African woman. They are strong, joyful, and loving, but are challenged beyond anyone's imagination. I am grateful for their inspiration and the good times we've spent together. Other contributors to this novel are the brilliant writings of Joseph Conrad and David Van Reybrouck. Also, traveling to Africa with Compassion International gave me a 3-D view of this beautiful continent and first hand experience of its people and the difficulties they face.

As always, I am grateful for the insight from the members of Window Pane, my writer's group in Vero Beach, Florida. My beta readers have been honest and thorough and for that I am grateful. They are: Kit Robey, Janet Sierzant, Charlene Lamb, Frank Langer, Don Mead, Carol Mead and Jon Den Houter. Their frankness and support have been invaluable. I give special thanks to Judi Konitzer for her willingness to smooth-out my prose and to catch the inconsistencies. She has been indispensable.

Thank you to my publishing company, Mission Point Press and its capable staff. Heather Shaw designed the cover, Bob Deck, the interior design, Susanne Dunlap did the editing, and Doug Weaver was the decision maker.

They were creative, professional and patient. I will always be grateful.

I must acknowledge those who are working the front lines in the Democratic Republic of the Congo. Dr. Denis Mukwege, received the Nobel Peace Prize in 2018 for his care of women who have been raped and sexually mutilated. He established the "City of Joy," which is a recovery treatment center. This program supports and heals those who are suffering from the aftermath of this terrible trauma. It is a redemptive mission because it transforms the mindset of the Congolese people and gives the victims newfound hope.

ABOUT THE AUTHOR

KATHRYN DEN HOUTER was a teacher and a psychologist for forty-five years. Currently, she is enjoying retirement and reading all the books on her wish list. Thirty years of her professional life were spent in Grand Rapids, Michigan. Here she parented four beautiful children with her late husband Len. They raised them on a hobby farm near Lowell, Michigan, a small town east of Grand Rapids. Her children: Jon, Jenna, Jessica, and Ben are embarking on their own careers. She has remarried and lives with her husband Jim. Their summer home is in Caledonia, Michigan and their winter home is in Indian River County, Florida. She delights in hearing from her readers. You can contact her through her email: kathryndenhouter@gmail.com, or her website kathryndenhouter.com.